COULD YOU BE WITH HER NOW

COULD YOU BE WITH HER NOW

two novellas

JEN MICHALSKI

DZANC BOOKS

DZANC BOOKS

1334 Woodbourne Street
Westland, MI 48186
www.dzancbooks.org

COULD YOU BE WITH HER NOW

Portions of "I Can Make It to California Before It's Time for Dinner" have appeared in *The Avatar Review* and *Lamination Colony*.

"May-September" was originally published in the *2010 Press 53 Awards Anthology*, first-place winner for novella.

Published 2013 by Dzanc Books
Design by Steven Seighman

ISBN: 978-1938103575
First edition: January 2013

ART WORKS.
arts.gov

michigan council for arts and cultural affairs

This project is supported in part by awards from the National Endowment for the Arts and Michigan Council for Arts and Cultural Affairs.

Printed in the United States of America

10   9   8   7   6   5   4   3   2   1

CONTENTS

Many thanks to Michael Kimball for his many thoughtful suggestions on the first draft; Barbara Westood Diehl, Lalita Noronha, Rosalia Scalia, Patricia Schultheis, and Todd Whaley for their suggestions on a subsequent draft, and Matt Bell for his masterful edits on the final draft of *I Can Make It to California before It's Time for Dinner*. Also, thanks to Amy Rodgers for awarding *May-September* First Prize (novella) in the Press 53 Open Awards (2010) and giving it the love and admiration I never thought it would see. Finally, thanks to Paula Bomer for being such an advocate for *May-September* in particular and my work in general; Dan and Steve at Dzanc for believing in my work, and Phuong Huynh and my family for believing in me.

I CAN MAKE IT TO CALIFORNIA BEFORE IT'S TIME FOR DINNER

1.

I watch the TV for my girlfriend Megan. She's fourteen and I am fifteen and every day she's on the show that I watch about her. She's pretty and I wish we could hold hands and kiss. My brother Josh is seventeen and doesn't play with me and doesn't like Megan. His girlfriend is not on TV and she's not pretty. Josh and his girlfriend call me retard and laugh. My name is Jimmy but I laugh too.

I am watching Megan on TV, but Josh wants to watch TV, too. He pushes me towards the door and then outside. He says, "Here's an idea—why don't you go find her?"

Josh knows I am only allowed to go to the 7-Eleven but he says maybe Megan lives somewhere between our house and the 7-Eleven. Maybe I will find her and kiss her. But the house Megan lives in on TV doesn't look like the houses on the way to 7-Eleven. Then I remember when we go to the Giant that the houses between our house and the Giant don't look the same as the houses between our house and the 7-Eleven and maybe those houses look like the house Megan lives in.

But I'm not allowed to walk to the Giant. It's too far.

I walk out of the yard.

Mr. Pete who drives the white truck is on the sidewalk. He is putting his big toolbox in the back. Once in the summer Mr. Pete gave me and Josh a ride to the skate park in the back of his truck. Josh tried to stand up on his skateboard while Mr. Pete was driving. He fell and Mr. Pete had to take us to the hospital because Josh broke his arm. Josh sat inside the truck then but I stayed in the back. The wind rushed into my mouth and I couldn't close it.

"Mr. Pete, do you know where Megan lives?" I ask.

"Can't say I do, Jimmy." He opens the door of his truck in, gets in.

"Do you think she lives near the Giant?"

"Not sure."

"Will you give me a ride to the Giant?"

"Your momma know you're going?"

He looks at me. His clothes are all white like Mr. Clean. But he doesn't have a bald head so he's not Mr. Clean's brother.

"You got a ride home?" he asks.

"Uh-huh."

He coughs into his hand and spits on the ground and he is thinking. "I gotta go, Jimmy—I'm late for work. Besides, I don't need to take no more Dembrowskis to the hospital."

I walk up the street. When we are in the car it doesn't take long to get to the Giant. It is one song on the radio, maybe two. But Megan doesn't live at the Giant. Dad says all the people on TV live in California. We live in Maryland. If I can make it to California before it's time for dinner, I should just probably go.

I walk and sing and I sing that Rihanna song four times and then Justin Timberlake three times. My feet hurt but I know I am getting closer to California. The houses are bigger than the one I live in with Josh and my mom and dad. I wonder if they're bigger because more people live in them.

There is one big brown and white house and it looks like Megan's house on TV but I can't remember exactly. I walk up to the door and knock but nobody answers. I hear music coming from behind the house. Behind the house the house has a deck. A girl is lying down in her bathing suit. She has brown hair like Megan and a body like Megan but Megan doesn't wear a bathing suit. It is her house I think so it must be her.

"Hi Megan."

I stand by the deck. The grass is growing over my sneakers and I smell dog poop. I wonder if Megan has a brother who mows the grass.

"Who are you?" She sits up. I can't see her eyes because she's wearing sunglasses.

"I'm Jimmy Dembrowski and I live on 890 Dunkirk and I watch you on TV."

"My name's not Megan," she says.

I walk up the steps so I can see her better.

"Stop right there." She holds up her hand. "You have to leave."

"I watch you on TV every day and you're pretty and I want to be your boyfriend."

"Do I look like I'm on TV?" She takes a sip of her soda.

"But people on TV are just like you and me." I say to her. "Can I have a soda?"

"Everything on TV is make-believe," she answers, lighting a cigarette. Megan doesn't smoke. "And no, you may not have a drink. You need to leave."

5

She stands and turns toward the house. There are glass doors and I can see myself behind her. "I'm going to tell you one more time to get out of here, and then I'm going to call the police."

I am on the deck now. I want to hug her goodbye. She pushes at me.

"Get away, you retard!" She screams and I put my hand on her mouth.

Megan bites my hand. I push her away. She is smaller than me and falls against the glass door. I feel bad and put my arms around her to pick her up. We are up half the way. She hits me in the chest and the face. I get mad like I get when Josh hits me and leaves marks. She hits me in the face again and it hurts bad. I put my hands on her neck and twist real hard, back and forth. She puts her hands on my hands but I am bigger. Her face turns all red and it's kind of funny how red. She keeps moving and kicking and I try to stop her. We are up half the way when she falls asleep on me. She is so heavy I let her fall and then I wait for her to stop make-believing because people on TV are always doing make-believe. The way Josh fake sleeps until I go away.

She make-believes her sleep and it is getting dark. It is time for dinner and I will get in trouble. I kiss Megan on the lips. I tell her I will see her tomorrow. At home I will tell Josh I found Megan out in California, that I kissed her, and that she does make-believe better than he does.

2.

I am walking through California and I am lost. I don't know any streets in California and I don't know any sidewalks in California and I don't know any houses in California and I don't know any people in California except for Megan. I wonder if she is still make-believing.

I walk to the end of the street. A dog is looking at me from his yard. It is across the street so I look both ways and cross. It is small like Peanut but not Peanut. Its fur is black and white and Peanut's is brown. The doggie smells my fingers through the fence. He licks them and I laugh. I want him to come home with me and then he and Peanut can get married and have puppies.

"Doodles! Come on Doodles!" A lady is calling the doggie. She doesn't look like my mom but she is somebody's mom. She walks down to the fence.

"He likes me," I say. "Do you know how to get back to Maryland?"

"Son, you are in Maryland." She frowns.

The lady leans over the fence. There is fat on her fingers and fat around her watch. She pushes the doggie behind her with her fat foot.

"Do you know where I live?" I ask.

"Are you lost?" She makes her face scrunch like Josh does when he is thinking.

I have a wallet in my pocket but it has no money because my mom keeps my allowance in a jar. But my wallet has my name on it, so I give it to her.

"Jimmy Dembrowski," she reads. "Well, Jimmy, why don't you come inside."

I nod and I want to pet Doodles again but Doodles is standing behind the lady sniffing her leg. "I'm going to give your parents a call."

Inside, the lady goes to the phone with my wallet and dials my number and the doggie sits by my leg and I pet it. The lady's living room smells different than our living room. I breathe out my mouth like I do sometimes when I am sick so I don't smell anymore. I pet the doggie. I wish I could take it with me. Maybe I can ask for it for Christmas. The lady hangs up the phone.

"Would you like a soda, Jimmy?"

I nod and the lady goes into the kitchen and gets a soda in a can. My mom won't let me drink soda from a can because she says I will cut my lip. I ask the lady to put it in a glass with ice please and she laughs and goes away with the soda can. I hold my nose with my hand so I can't smell and then I am breathing more through my mouth.

The lady comes back with my soda.

"Is there something wrong?" The lady hands me a cup with soda and ice.

"It smells funny," I say.

Mom says to hold my cup with both hands when I drink so I don't spill. But I'm holding my nose with my hand so I hold the cup in one hand. The TV is on but Megan is not on because it is not time for Megan to be on TV. She was on TV before now and she will be on tomorrow and I will be home and I will watch her.

"I saw my girlfriend Megan," I tell the lady.

I am holding the glass and I am holding my nose and my voice sounds funny and I giggle. I drop my cup and there is soda on the floor. The doggie licks the soda off the floor with his pink tongue and I laugh. Mom gets mad when I drop things. I hope the lady doesn't tell her. The lady yells at the doggie and tries to move it away from the soda. I sit very still and try not to laugh. The lady says a bad word.

"That's a bad word," I say.

The lady shakes her head and goes in the kitchen and says the word again. I can hear it but I don't tell her.

3.

"Thank you, lady!" I say it because Mom tells me to.

I hug the doggie. I am going to miss him but I am not going to miss the lady. I get in the car in the back and Mom gets in the front on her side and Dad gets in on his side.

"Jimmy, how did you get out here?" Mom asks.

"I walked."

"All that way?" Mom's eyes get wide. "Your brother is going to get it."

"I went to see my girlfriend Megan."

Mom and Dad look at each other but don't say anything.

At home we sit on the sofa like we do for big talks.

"That lady's house smelled. Pee-yew." I put my hand on my nose and laugh.

"Jimmy, this is very serious. Do you want a spanking?"

"I'm too big for a spanking." I sit on my hands and rock back and forth. From the armchair Josh hides behind his hands but I can see the funny face he's making and I try not to giggle.

"Okay, then stop laughing. This is very serious. You know you are only allowed to go to the 7-Eleven and back. You are not to ask for rides from anybody, you understand? Not even Mr. Pete. You are not to go anywhere without telling me or your father or Josh where you are going. You could have gotten hit by a car or worse."

"But Josh told me to go!"

"And Josh has been punished for it. Now, you repeat after me: I am not allowed to go anywhere except the 7-Eleven. I must tell Mom or Dad or Josh where I am going."

"Mom, I'm hungry."

"We're all hungry, Jimmy. We searched all over the neighborhood for you, and then we get a call from a woman on the other side of town. You have to promise Mommy that you will not do that again, you hear me?"

"Yes, Mommy."

"Turd," Josh says in his quiet voice to me.

I laugh because turd is a bad word, but Dad gives me a look. I run into the kitchen and hide behind Peanut.

Mom calls for pizza on the telephone and I am excited because we are having pizza and it isn't Friday. Mom and Dad are talking in the kitchen. Dad fixes toilets and sometimes he tells me he will fix me. He gets up for work before I do for school and he comes home after I do. I see him on the weekends because he watches TV in the living room. I know he is mad at me and he's mad at Josh and he's mad at Mom, too, and it's all my fault.

Mom hands me a napkin.

"It's okay, Jimmy—don't cry. Nobody got hurt. Stop crying or you won't get your soda."

"He doesn't need any soda." Dad sits at the table and opens the newspaper. "You want him bouncing off the walls and getting into more trouble?"

I don't like it when Mom and Dad fight. When we have pizza on Friday we are happy except sometimes like when Mom got laid off from her job. Then we didn't have pizza for a long time.

Maybe Josh will play with me until the pizza comes. But the door of our room is locked.

"Go away," he says.

I knock and knock until he opens the door. I stomp my feet on the floor and laugh. "I went to California and you didn't!"

He goes back into our room and I go too.

"What the hell were you doing going across town like that? You know I got grounded for two weeks because of you? Why can't you just keep out of trouble and not be so retarded?"

"I'm sorry. I'm a stupe."

I shake my head to shake the stupid out. I will be as smart as Josh. I will go to Josh's school and maybe we can sit next to each other and do finger-paints of army men.

"I'm a stupe, stupe." I hit my head hard with my hand.

"Jesus, would you fucking stop it. Just sit down and chill out for once. You want Dad to come up and let us both have it?"

I sit down on Josh's bed.

"Your bed's not made," I say, laughing.

"Your head's not made. Sit on your own bed."

I jump on my own bed and pull my sheets over my head. I make-believe sleep but I am not good at it.

"Don't do anything like that again. I can't get in any more trouble."

"I'm sorry. I don't want Mom and Dad to be mad at you."

"Okay, fine. I forgive you, okay? Just don't go anywhere without me. Even if I tell you to."

"Josh?"

"Yeah, Jimmy?"

"Can I have your crusts when the pizza comes?"

4.

I pretend I'm a dinosaur eating people. Dad tells me to eat with my mouth closed because I'm not a cow. I put my napkin over my mouth to laugh in it but Dad is too busy getting paper towels and Mom is too busy putting more soda in my glass to yell at me.

"Peanut," I call. "Peanut! You want some pizza, Peanut?"

"Shut up, Jimmy." Josh looks at me mean. "You know it gives her the shits. And look who always has to clean it up because you're too retarded to do anything."

I throw a piece of crust at him.

"Mom!" Josh yells. "Jimmy wants to get into even more trouble tonight!"

"I didn't do anything."

God can hear lies but I said it real quiet. No one should commit a sin or lie because they will go to hell. I am scared of hell and I don't want to lie but I don't want to be yelled at again because it's pizza night.

I get ready for bed. Josh is watching TV in our room. He is being quiet so Mom doesn't tell him to turn it off. I am playing with my army men, Grunt and Sergeant Slaughter. They are brave and fight for our country and I want to be in the army when I grow up. Then I can shoot people but only bad people because we are the good guys. USA! And everybody that fights against the USA are bad guys. So I will shoot them. Josh says I am not smart enough to get in the army but I think he is wrong. I think when I am bigger I will be smarter.

"That's my girlfriend!" My girlfriend Megan is on the TV but it is not the show I watch about her. It is the news. I bounce on my bed because Megan is on TV.

Josh looks at me. "Dude, that girl is dead. She's not your girlfriend."

"I saw her today. She make-believed her sleep."

"Well, apparently she wasn't pretending. She's dead."

Josh stands in front of the TV and I can't see Megan anymore.

"Jimmy, did you really meet this girl today? What were you doing out in Kingsville, anyway?"

"I wasn't in Kingsville, Josh." I roll my eyes because sometimes Josh does not listen. "I was in California."

"You were not. You know how far away California is, stupid? You'd have to get on a plane and fly there, and it'd still take you eight hours. Remember when we visited Disneyland, how long it took?"

"But I saw her. I saw Megan from TV. Josh, you are not made of glass."

Josh moves, but Megan is gone. "Did you see Megan from TV, or did you see that girl just on the TV?"

"I don't know. I don't remember."

"Jimmy, this is important. Did you or did you not see that girl today?"

"Are you mad at me?"

"Jimmy, I'm not mad at you. I'm just trying to figure this out."

"Figure what out?"

"What happened between you and that girl." Josh walks back and forth. I do, too, because it's funny. "Stop—this is serious. Okay, so if you did see this girl, you just talked to her. She got mad at you, and a lot of people do that." He sits down in front of his computer. "Don't say anything to anyone about today, okay?"

"I'm sorry you got in trouble."

"Jimmy, put your pajamas on." I have the blanket over my head and make-believe sleep. "And brush your teeth."

I make a sound but I am not sad because I like my pajamas. They have army men on them.

5.

It is time for school. Some of the kids on our block say I go to a retard school, but Mom says that they are jealous. Josh goes to the school for bigger kids. If he went to my school too he would have to learn twice. Today we are learning about adding tables and yesterday we are learning about adding tables but I don't know about tomorrow. I know that three plus one is four and three plus two is five and three plus three is six but I don't know after. Last night Mom was supposed to help me with my homework but we had pizza and she forgot and I forgot.

We learn about how to dial 911 on the telephone if we need help. But it has to be a really big kind of help because I asked my teacher Mrs. Rawlings if I can call 911 if I need help getting my shoe off and she said no. I asked Mrs. Rawlings can I call 911 if I didn't do my homework and she said no. I asked her what if I hit a girl and she make-believes sleep? Mrs. Rawlings said I should call my parents or family member because someone would be home with me at all times. Mrs. Rawlings asked me if someone was home with me at all times and I said yes. I asked

Mrs. Rawlings can I call 911 if Peanut gets out of the yard and she said that I had asked enough questions. Then I had one more question I said what if I get lost? And she said yes so maybe the next time I can't find my way home I can call 911 and not have to sit in the lady's house.

Mrs. Rawlings is a black lady and she is nice. I am not black because my parents are white. My Dad doesn't call black people black. He calls them something else but I am not allowed to repeat it. Mom tells me never, ever to call Mrs. Rawlings that word or tell her I know of it. Mom tells me to pretend that word is pretend, but I can't.

Sometimes when Mom tells me not to do something I feel like I'm going to blow up because I keep thinking about the thing. Like if Mom told me before school not to say the word asshole I feel like I will blow up and I will feel better if I say asshole at the top of my voice to shout it out of me but I can't. And that's how I got in trouble with the word Dad calls black people. We were in the mall and I said it to a black man and my mother slapped me and then I felt like I was going to blow up. But I didn't say it again.

But sometimes I'm afraid I will say a word I don't want to. It will just come out of my mouth and I didn't mean it. Josh told me that if I wanted to say a bad word I should just shout blue because no one can punish you for that.

Mrs. Rawlings gave us a card with 911 on it so we can call it if we're lost. I put it in my wallet with my other card. I asked Mom why I can give strangers the card with my name on it but not tell them my name. She said not to show the card to anybody but a policeman. I showed my card to the lady yesterday. And if I call 911, I have to give them my name. But Mom says not to talk to strangers, not even Mr. Pete.

I get in trouble at school for not having my homework. I tell Mrs. Rawlings that it was pizza night but I don't tell her about California because Josh told me not to. Mrs. Rawlings says that pizza is not a reason for not having my homework done. She gives me extra homework and she also gives me a note to take home to my Mom and Dad. I have never been in trouble before.

Mrs. Rawlings tells me not to cry, that everybody gets in trouble sometimes.

Even superheroes and army men? I ask. She does not hear me.

6.

Josh picks me up at school. He has his own car. Sometimes Josh lets me pretend drive when he is getting gas. I drive the cars at the arcade but Josh says I drive like an old lady. I tell him I don't want to crash but all the cars go by me and I lose.

"Jimmy, did you tell anybody about yesterday?" he asks when I get in the car.

"No. And I got in trouble because I didn't do my homework."

He pulls away from my school. "I don't think anybody knows you were in Kingsville yesterday, so no one is going to bother you and ask you questions and you're not going to concoct some crazy story."

"I don't concoct crazy stories, Josh." I laugh.

"But you killed your gerbil, remember?"

I am sad because I loved Mr. Kibble. I would take him out of the cage and hold him and he would feed out of my hand. One night I took him out of his cage because I wanted him to sleep with me even though Mom told me he could not sleep with me.

He was warm and furry and his heart beat very fast and I hugged him because he was warm.

But when I woke up the next day Mr. Kibble was under my tummy on the bed and he was cold. Josh laughed and laughed because I fell asleep on him but I cried.

Dad wouldn't let us get a Mr. Kibble Two because he said I would just kill it. Mr. Kibble is buried in the backyard in a box and Mom says he is protecting us from intruders. I want Mr. Kibble's box to be buried under my bed so he would protect me from the bad guys but Dad says if I dig Mr. Kibble out of the backyard I will get a beating I will never forget.

"Shit, look."

Josh is pointing at our yard. There is a police car in the driveway. I like policemen because they protect me. But Josh does not park the car. He keeps going.

"Where are you going, Josh? Why don't we go home?"

"Because if that cop sees that nobody is home, then he'll leave. We'll just wait for him to leave."

"But I want to see him."

"We're going to go to the 7-Eleven and get Slurpees, and then we'll come back, okay?"

We go to the 7-Eleven and I ask Josh to buy me baseball cards because I don't have any money. It's in my allowance jar at home and I have to tell Mom what I'm using my money for. Once Josh's friend Steve said that if I didn't pay him my allowance every week that bullies would beat me up. It worked because nobody beat me up but then Mom got mad and Josh got punished.

Josh never buys me cards when I ask him but today he does. And a Slurpee, too. I like my Slurpee so that it's coke and grape together. Josh makes my Slurpee for me because once I tried to make one by myself and I got it all over my clothes.

We drive back to our house and the policeman is gone. Josh doesn't pull into our driveway but parks on the street. He tells me to get in the house fast so nobody sees us. I pretend I'm in the army and make rifle noises as I run into the house and up the stairs. Josh tells me to stay in our room and not to come out.

I look at my baseball cards and I put them into my baseball card locker by team and then by position. I got one new card, Brandon Inge of the Detroit Tigers. The rest are doubles, but I keep them because I don't have anybody to trade them with. I am done with my baseball cards and so I drink my Slurpee. I put my notebook on my desk and I pretend I am writing code in the army like I saw on the GI Joe cartoon.

Josh closes the door and puts a finger to his lips.

"Dad just got home. I told him you were playing at Tommy Jenkins' house."

"But I don't like Tommy Jenkins. He calls me names."

"Never mind that. Dad's going over to the Jenkins' house now. I need to get you out of here while he's gone."

"Why?"

"Because the police told Dad that they got a description of a retarded boy around that girl's house yesterday afternoon."

"But I didn't do anything!"

"We need time to think of a story for you. So you're going to go behind the high school, where we used to play pogs with the other kids. Just stay there until I come get you. Go now."

"I have to pack." I take my backpack and put my homework in it and my army men.

"Here's ten dollars." Josh says.

It is a lot of money, more than my allowance.

"If you get hungry waiting, go over to the McDonald's to get something to eat. I'm going to feel Dad out when he gets back, and then I'll come and get you."

"But you told me not to go anywhere without you."

"This is different."

"What if I get lost?"

"You know where both the McDonald's and the school is. How are you going to get lost?"

"But you said..."

"It doesn't matter. Just go. Go the back way. Go now. Wait there for me, got it?"

7.

I walk to Josh's school, where we play pogs. I wish I brought my pogs because maybe those kids will be there. I go behind the school. I have homework for tomorrow but I will do it later because I can't write on the ground. I bring out my army men from my backpack and I play with Grunt and Sergeant Slaughter and I am Private Jimmy. We will fight the bad guys, win against the bad guys. POW! POW!

I am done playing. I lie in the grass like sleeping and look at the clouds. One day Mrs. Rawlings took us outside for recess and we looked at the clouds. She said that clouds look like things sometimes. Mrs. Rawlings saw a bunny once. I don't see any bunny even though I look hard. I wonder if I will be able to see them when I'm bigger. I don't want to look at clouds anymore or play GI Joes and there are no pog kids. I stand up and go around in a circle.

I go around and I fall down because the ground is going and the school is going but I am not going. When the ground and the school stop going I get up and start going in a circle again. I look up at the clouds again to see if they are going. They are, but they are still clouds.

I am hungry. I could get a Quarter Pounder and fries and a chocolate shake at McDonald's with the money Josh gave me. I put my homework and GI Joes in my backpack and I walk to the McDonald's. I go to the counter and ask for a Quarter Pounder, fries, and a chocolate shake please. I give them the ten bill and they give me money back. I can get more food if I am hungry again.

The lady at the counter asks me to move to the side to wait for my order. I look at the pictures of the burgers and fries and chicken nuggets. The lady gives me my shake and I go to find a straw. When I get back the lady tells me not to leave my money on the counter because somebody might take it so I put it in my pocket.

My food comes. I am very happy because last night we had pizza even though it wasn't Friday and today I had McDonald's even though it is not my birthday.

I get three cups of ketchup. I dip each fry in the ketchup and then I eat the fry. Josh says I eat like a dork but Dad says Josh eats like a pig. I would rather be a dork than a pig.

I finish my Quarter Pounder and french fries and shake. I go to the counter and I order chicken nuggets, french fries, and another chocolate shake but the lady tells me I don't have enough money. But this is all I have I say and she says she will change my order to the small nuggets and small fries and regular shake.

She asks me what kind of sauces I would like for my nuggets and I tell her I don't know. She asks me if I like barbecue and I tell her yes. She gives me barbecue. I open the barbecue packet and eat it and the lady says those are for your nuggets. I tell her I don't like barbecue can I please have another? She gives me honey mustard and says save this for your nuggets don't eat it.

I drink my shake and my stomach hurts a little. My nuggets are ready. The lady picks my money off the counter and hands it to me. I pull out my wallet and put it on the counter. I pull out my money and it falls on the floor. I bend over and get the quarter and another quarter and one penny, one penny, one penny but I can't find the other penny.

"Did you see the penny?" I ask the man behind me and he shakes his head.

I get on my hands and knees like I did when we looked for Josh's contact that he puts in his eye to see and I look for the penny. I crawl and people in the line get out of my way and someone laughs. I find the penny all the way on the other side then I bring the money back to the counter.

The lady tells me to move to the side to put it in my wallet so I do. I put the two quarters and one, two, three, four pennies in the change purse.

"I have money in my wallet." I tell the lady.

"I wouldn't tell that to everybody you meet," she says.

I put my wallet on my tray and walk to my booth but a man is sitting in it. He is eating two hamburgers and is fat.

"That is my booth."

"I didn't see your name on it."

"You don't have to write your name on the seat at McDonald's," I say, but I remember that my desk at school has my name on it with a picture of an army man. "Do you?"

The man laughs and points to the booth across from him that is not my booth. If Mrs. Rawlings was here I would tell on him. I sit in the booth across from the man in my booth. I dip a nugget in the honey mustard dipping sauce. I like it better than the barbecue so I dip my chicken nuggets in it and put my tongue in it to get all the sauce out. I dip my French Fries in the ketchup but then I feel sick.

My tummy hurts and I feel sick like when I stay home from school and throw up. I put both hands on my stomach to push it back but I feel it come up and onto the table.

"Jesus Christ!" The man who is sitting in my booth says.

He gets up and leaves. Then a man comes and tells me I need to leave so he can clean up. I sit in my booth and watch him.

"Why don't you put dirt on it?" I ask. He doesn't answer.

I get up to say goodbye to the lady at the counter. The lady smiles and gives me a Happy Meal toy even though I didn't get a Happy Meal.

"Can I have another one?" I ask.

A man with a tie stands behind her. His arms are crossed.

"Son, are you here with someone?" he asks.

"No. My brother Josh is picking me up." I answer. "Can I have another toy?"

"Why don't you wait for your brother in front of the store?" the man says. The lady smiles and gives me a little wave.

Outside it is becoming night. I rip open the Happy Meal bag. It is the Batman but I have this Batman so I walk across the street. I leave him in the middle of the street. The cars go and go and go by him but they do not hit him because he is the Batman.

8.

Night is when bad guys wake up and hurt people. I have Sergeant Slaughter and Grunt. I hold them close.

"You guys need to protect me," I say.

I am walking down the street I know. I cannot see the clouds anymore. They must be sleeping. I see a balloon and another balloon and then I see balloons all in the sky. It is like at school when we put tags on balloons with our names on them and we get a prize if our balloon goes the longest away.

I did not know balloons come out at night. I only see them during the day. Maybe they are balloons that wake up when it becomes night. I have to ask Mrs. Rawlings. She is home with her mommy or maybe she is a mommy. If I tell her tomorrow I saw balloons outside at night she will say I'm making things up again. Like when I told her my dad had a chicken in his pants. He doesn't have a chicken in his pants, she told me, but I said he says there is a cock. Our flashcard with the chicken on it says *cock*. It makes some boys laugh. It makes me laugh too because I think it's funny that Dad has a chicken in his pants.

I see balloons a lot. They are walking across the sky the other way and I follow them. I wonder if they are out late and they are going home and their mommies will be mad at them. I walk with the balloons walking above me. We are a parade and it makes me happy.

The balloons move fast so I walk fast. But it becomes night and it is hard to see them in the dark. Some balloons are caught on the telephone pole lines that bring TV to our house. I am sad because they are getting left behind. I yell at the other balloons to come back but they don't hear me.

I am running after the balloons and I am looking at the sky and then I am on the ground because I did not see the part of the sidewalk where it is broken. Sergeant Slaughter and Grunt are okay but my hands hurt and my knee hurts and my shoulder hurts.

I should go home so my mom can blow on my scrapes and put band-aids on them. I don't know the street that I am on. I do not see the balloons.

I see some of these stores and buildings when I am in Mom's car but I don't know how to get home. Maybe I can find a telephone and use my card with my name and phone number on it. I reach into my pocket for my wallet but it's not there. I turn around on the sidewalk to go back to McDonald's but it looks different and I don't know where to go. I feel tears in my eyes but I am not a baby. I am brave. I am going to be in the army.

Mrs. Rawlings said I can call 911 if I'm lost. Then the police will come. But Josh says that policemen don't protect me anymore. Maybe I can ask someone to take me home, but Mom says not to talk to strangers. Josh says things and then he says other things and I don't know what to do.

9.

My legs are tired and they want to sleep and so do I. I am mad at Josh but when I get home I won't hate him because he is my brother. God hears everything I say so I love Josh, love Josh, love Josh. Also, God, please I am lost and I need a telephone and a puppy for Christmas.

I see a gas station where there are lots of trucks with a lot of wheels and I am happy because they have big horns and maybe I will hear them. I walk up to a big truck. It is silver with lightning bolts. It looks like a truck I have in my toy chest.

I laugh at the man in the truck. "Honk, honk, honk!"

"Honk the horn?" The man laughs. He is wearing a hat with the word CAT on it. "I'll scare half the gas station. Gotta get out on the highway, you gonna blow the horn."

"Honk the horn!"

I laugh and pull my arm up and honk the horn but I am not honking I am pretending. The man gets out of his truck. He is short and fat like a Weeble and has a moustache like Yosemite Sam, but he is not a cartoon he is a real man.

"Are you by yourself here, boy?"

"Yes, but I am calling 911 because I'm lost."

"Lost? Where do you live, son?"

"I live at 890 Dunkirk."

"Well, what's your name?"

"Jimmy Dembrowski."

"Well, Jimmy, I know how to get you home."

"You do? But I don't know you."

"I can know where you live, son. That's what maps are for. Hop in and I'll have you home before your momma gets worried."

"Can I honk the horn?" I ask.

"Well, we'll have to get on the highway to do that. But then I'll take you home. How does that sound?"

"Okay."

"Well, all right. Welcome to Big Thunder. I'm Ed."

I climb in Big Thunder. Trucks have names like people but not people names. A rubber frog is hanging around the mirror that helps you look backward. There is also a little green tree that makes a car smell like a tree. There are maps on the seat and I move them so I don't sit on them. The man Ed gets in his side of the truck. "All right, Jimmy. Buckle up."

I put on my seatbelt and he starts the truck. I am happy because I'm going home and because I get to honk the horn. We are driving on the big road. We drive on the big road when we are going to the beach or when we go to Aunt Sissy and Uncle Dave's. The big road goes far away but it also goes home.

"Can I honk the horn now?" I turn to ask Mr. Ed.

"Almost, Jimmy boy. You wanna hear some music? Some honky-tonk? Some Hank Williams Sr?"

Mr. Ed starts singing and I laugh because he sings like Dad.

"Come on, Jimmy—*Hey, I left my home down on a rural route, Told my folks' I'm goin' stampin' out, and get the honky-tonk blues!*"

"Honky-tonk blues!"

"Hey Lord, I got 'em."

"Honky-tonk blues!"

"That's good, Jimmy. You're a natural."

"Can I honk the horn now?"

"I don't see why not. Reach on over and give 'er a pull."

I pull on the horn and it's loud. I laugh and pull it again.

"Okay, that's enough. Don't want anybody to think we're honkin' at them, now do we?" Mr. Ed winks at me.

"Now, you like lollipops? I got lollipops. A whole bag of them."

I nod.

"Well, okay, open the glove compartment and get yourself one out."

"Can I have two?"

"One for now, one for later? Good thinking, Jimmy. Go ahead."

I open the glove compartment and get a purple lollipop and a red lollipop. I don't know which one I want first. I unwrap each one and I lick each one back and forth. They taste good. My favorite candy is Tootsie Rolls. I put a lot of them in my mouth and chew and Josh says I look like I'm eating turds. When I go trick or treating with my classmate Henry I trade my candy corns and my Snickers for his Tootsie Rolls. I like Snickers but I like Tootsie Rolls tops. Every year I am an army soldier.

"Mr. Ed, I want to go home now. I live at 890 Dunkirk."

"Okay. So how do I get there?"

"I don't know!" I throw my lollipop stick on the floor of the truck. "You told me you could take me home!"

"Don't be mad, Jimmy. We'll figure it out." Mr. Ed hands me his handkerchief and I wipe my tears. He pats my shoulder. "Tired, son? Listen, I got a bed up there in the cab. Why don't you lie down and take a nap? Before you know it, you'll be home. I promise."

"You will wake me up when we get home?"

"Scout's honor." He puts his hand over his heart like he is saying the pledge of allegiance.

There is a door behind the seat and then there is a room with a bed. I climb in bed. Mr. Ed does not have army men on his sheets. He has grown-up sheets instead.

I close my eyes and say my prayers. I tell God that when I get bigger I am going to drive a truck on the big roads and I am going to have a bed and be friends with Sergeant Slaughter and Grunt and maybe have a hamster, Mr. Kibble Two.

10.

I wake up and I don't know where I am. I remember that I'm in Mr. Ed's truck. I cannot wait until school because then I can tell Mrs. Rawlings and Henry and Steven and the girl in the wheelchair about Mr. Ed and his truck. The girl in the wheelchair can't walk but she can ride in the bus when we go to the zoo because the bus puts the wheelchair in the bus. If the girl in the wheelchair was riding in the truck with me and Mr. Ed, the truck would have to put her in the truck. Then I would show her the bed and I would ask Mr. Ed if she could honk the horn.

I get out of the bed and climb into the front of the truck. I open the glove compartment and pull out a lollipop. But then I hide it because I worry he is going to yell at me like Dad because I didn't ask first.

"Good morning, Jimmy."

Mr. Ed looks funnier in the morning. He has a mustache but also a beard that is not a beard, like the one my Dad shaves off in the morning.

"Did you sleep good?"

"Yes. But I have to go to school now and I didn't do my homework so I'm going to get in trouble."

"Don't worry about school today, Jim."

I unwrap the lollipop. I will not tell Mom I had lollipops for breakfast. "I have school on Monday, Tuesday, Wednesday, Thursday, and Friday."

"Here's the thing, Jimmy. I got this important delivery to make, down in Florida. It's so important that I don't have time to drop you back home first. So I'm going to make this delivery, and you're going to be my first mate, like on a ship, helping me to deliver this cargo. And then I'll take you home. How's that sound?"

I scratch my head and smell my fingers. Mom washes my hair every Monday, Wednesday, Friday, and Sunday. But I was not home last night. I was sleeping in the truck. "I want to go home. I don't want to miss school."

"I talked to your mom, and she says it's okay. She talked to your school, and everything is going to be okay."

"I won't get in trouble for missing school?"

"Nope."

"I want to talk to Mom first."

"She's going to call us back later. She had things to do this morning."

"Oh. Okay. Mr. Ed? I'm hungry. Do you have more than lollipops?"

Mr. Ed looks in the frog mirror and rubs his chin beard. "All right, Jimmy. There's a place that's about twenty miles down the road. Can you wait until then?"

I look at the big road so I don't hear my tummy talk.

"What games do you play on the big road, Mr. Ed? When we go on the big road to the beach Mom plays games with us."

Mr. Ed scratches his head. He scratches his head because he

is thinking, not because it tickles or because it smells. I asked Josh once why people scratch their head when it's not a tickle and he said they do it when they're thinking. So I scratched my head when I was thinking all the time and then it hurt. Mom said I scratched my head too much and it was bleeding. She said to scratch my head only when it itches.

"I'm by myself on the road, so I sing," he says. "Sometimes I listen to books on tape."

"Mr. Ed, does this road go to the beach?"

"Sure. This road runs next to the Atlantic coast."

"Can we go to the beach?"

"Maybe, Jimmy, if we have some time. We'll have to make this important delivery first. We're in South Carolina now. We won't get to Florida until late tonight. Then we can go to the beach. Lots of beaches in Florida. Ever been to Florida? They got Miami Beach, Palm Beach. They got Disneyworld there. You been to Disneyworld?"

"I went to Disneyland in California. I saw Mickey Mouse and Donald Duck and Pluto. I went on a lot of rides and I got a t-shirt and a stuffed Buzz Lightyear. I like Buzz Lightyear. Can we go to Disneyworld?"

"Nah, we won't have the time for both."

"But we'll see?"

I am happy. I am riding in the truck. Maybe if I'm good Mr. Ed will let me honk the horn again. But I miss Mom and Josh and Mrs. Rawlings and I miss my house and I miss Megan. Maybe she won't be mad at me anymore. I will be sorry for being mad and putting my hands on her like when Josh and I play.

But Josh says Megan on the TV is not the same Megan in the yard. Once when we were at Disneyland Josh told me that the Mickey Mouse at Disneyland was not the Mickey Mouse I saw on TV. I told him he was a liar and Mom told me not to listen

35

to him but he said it's true. I said if that's true when I am on the videotape of my birthday party it's not me? Of course it's you, he says. It's just you on the videotape. So I think he is lying when he says the Mickey Mouse I hugged was not the one on TV.

Besides, Josh told me to wait for him at the school and not stay home and wait for Dad and now I am riding in the truck with Mr. Ed to Florida. Josh thinks he is really smart but I don't think he's as smart as he thinks he is. I think that when I get bigger, I will be smarter than him.

11.

The truck slows down. There is sign that says W-A-F-F-L-E H-O-U-S-E and we are going to have breakfast. But then I remember I don't have my wallet with the money that Josh gave me. When I start to cry, Mr. Ed shows me his wallet. It is big and black and looks like it has lots of money in it.

"Breakfast is on me, Jimmy."

"Can I have eggs and pancakes and sausage and orange juice?"

"Sure can." Mr. Ed climbs out of the truck. He looks like Uncle Stewart. Uncle Stewart is fat and he has a mustache that frowns. He smells like Uncle Stewart too. When I smell like Mr. Ed and Mr. Stewart, Mom tells me to take a bath. I wish I could tell Josh how short and fat Mr. Ed is, like Uncle Stewart. Maybe I can call him on the phone but right now I am hungry.

I will eat a lot today and I won't throw up because I'll chew my food a lot the way Mom tells me to. I go to the long table with the chairs without backs. I sit on one and spin around and laugh. I watch Mr. Ed sit down and pull his handkerchief out of his pocket. He blows his nose and honks.

"What can I get ya?" The lady who makes our food asks.

"Gimmee a short stack, some eggs over easy, double sausage, and a coffee."

Mr. Ed does not look at the menu so I don't, either. "What do you want, Jimmy?"

"I want pancakes and an Egg McMuffin and orange juice."

"This ain't McDonald's, hon. How do you want them eggs? In a sandwich?"

"I like them like Mom does."

"Well, honey, I'm not your mother." The lady laughs. She is not Mom but she is someone else's mom because she is old like Mom but not as pretty. She is also fat and has a spot on her face that's big and brown and round. It looks like a bug without legs. I wonder if she cries because she has a spot on her face.

"My mom makes me eggs and they look like that."

I point to the man next to me. He's eating the eggs that my mom makes.

"Hey, I like your eggs. I like eggs like that, too!"

"Leave the man alone, Jimmy." Mr Ed. says.

"It's okay," the man with my eggs says. "They call these scrambled, son."

"Scrambled egg!"

I hit my head. Some people scratch their head when they think and some people hit their head when they remember things. "I like my eggs scrambled, please."

"That your son?" the man asks Mr. Ed.

"No," I explain to him. "Mr. Ed is not my dad. Mr. Ed picked me up at the gas station last night."

"Okay, Jimmy. That's enough."

Mr. Ed holds his hand up. He is acting like Dad, who always yells at me, even when I'm not doing anything. The woman who has the bug spot on her face comes back and gives Mr. Ed his coffee and me my orange juice. I drink all of my orange juice because I am thirsty.

I watch Mr. Ed drink his coffee. He takes big drinks and when you get bigger you drink coffee. I am pretending I drive a truck like Mr. Ed so maybe I should get coffee, too. But then our food comes and I forget because I have pancakes and scrambled eggs and sausage.

Mr. Ed pats his face with a napkin, which means he is finished eating. If he is my dad, he is going to fart next and my mother will yell at him and Josh and I will laugh.

"Hurry up, Jimmy."

"Are you going to fart?" I ask.

"What? Hurry up now. We gotta get on the road. Deliveries to make."

I am not done with my breakfast. I don't want to eat it fast because I don't want to throw up. I take a napkin and I roll a sausage in it and then I take a pancake and put it on a napkin and then I pour syrup on it but the counter gets sticky because not all the syrup stayed on the napkin. I put another napkin on top of the pancake and then I get a napkin for the rest of my eggs.

"Son, you're making a mess," Mr. Ed says. "Can we get a box over here?"

The bug lady gives me a box to put my food in. I unroll the sausage and put it in the box and then I put the pancake in the box and pour more syrup in it. Then I put a napkin in the box between the sausage and the pancake so that sausage does not get syrup on it but the napkin has syrup all over it so I put another napkin over top of it. Mr. Ed pays the check and I wave goodbye to the bug lady and the scrambled egg man.

When I get home I'm going to tell Josh I ate at the big table. This is the first time I've been away for a whole overnight. I went on an overnight to my friend Henry's before. Mom packed my army men pajamas and my toys and I was excited. We ate pizza even though it was not Friday and played army men and put our sleeping bags in Henry's basement. But when Henry's mom turned the light off I got scared even though she brought Henry's night light down and then I missed Mom and Josh and my own bed and I cried and cried until Henry's mom called my mom and she came to pick me up. I rode in the car in my pajamas and mom said I fell asleep in the front seat. If I have to stay overnights again, maybe it would be okay if we slept in our car.

12.

Mr. Ed's truck is louder than our car. It is the daytime and I can see the big road good. It's fun because we're tall and I can look down at the other cars. They look smaller than when I am in our car. It is weird that things get smaller when you are not close to them but they really do not get small. I wonder if Mom would be small now if I saw her.

One two three four lanes of cars go our way and one two three four of cars go the other way. There are people in those cars and they live in houses and have mommies and daddies and some are mommies and daddies and some have dogs and some have cats. I bet there are so many people in the world I couldn't count them all on my fingers but it is a lot like when we go to the baseball game. I tried to count the people at the game but I can only count to twenty and then I counted to twenty five times and then Dad told me to be quiet because he was watching the game and then Mom took me for a hot dog. And then we did the wave. I will never forget that day.

"Bear in the air, 95 and 20. Anybody copy?"

The little walkie-talkie on Mr. Ed's dashboard is talking. Mr. Ed picks it up.

"Big Thunder, copy. Ten-4," Mr. Ed says into the box and puts it back.

"Mr. Ed, what is that?"

"It's a CB." Mr. Ed holds it up toward me. "It's like walkie-talkie for trucks."

"Is there a bear in the sky?"

I look out the window but all I see are clouds. Not even clouds that look like bears.

"No." Mr. Ed laughs. "It's just CB lingo. It's like a secret language for truckers."

"Like army men have code?"

"We can find out about road conditions from other truckers or where the cops are hiding. 'Bear in the air' actually means there's a police helicopter around the intersection of Interstates 95 and 20. That way, I know to be going double-nickel, or 55 miles per hour, so I won't get stopped by the cops."

"But the police have walkie-talkies, too! I saw them!"

"Yeah, but their CBs don't use the same frequency."

Mr. Ed puts the CB back on the dashboard. It still talks, but Mr. Ed doesn't answer anymore. He yawns.

"Can I talk in the CB?"

"No, Jimmy. This is a secret mission."

Mr. Ed puts his hand in his pocket and pulls out a pill. He sticks it in his mouth and takes a swig of soda. It is the second pill he takes today. I bet he has a really bad headache. He asks me how I got to the gas station and I tell him.

"You're not making any of this up, son?" Mr. Ed pushes a stick on the floor to make the truck go faster. "This ain't some big story?"

I shake my head and Mr. Ed makes the radio loud so we can't hear the CB anymore. Mr. Ed doesn't look like a dad. But neither does Uncle Stewart. And Dad and Uncle Stewart don't look alike even though they are brothers. And Josh and I don't look alike even though we are brothers. Josh's hair is blond and long and mine is short and brown. Whenever I ask Mom if I can grow my hair long like Josh she says I'd have to wash it more.

I pick a sausage out of my box and eat it. It's still warm. I don't have sausage every day, only if we go out to eat. I eat cereal every day before school. I like Lucky Charms the best.

I eat all the marshmallows first. Sometimes I don't want to eat the other pieces but Mom says I have to. Sometimes I feed them to Peanut. Once I put them in my pocket before school but I forgot about them and when Mom washed my clothes they got all over my clothes and Mom got mad. After that, she bought raisin bran but then she bought Lucky Charms again because I fed Peanut my raisins and then he pooped all over the house.

"What's so funny, Jimmy?"

"Once I fed my dog Peanut some raisins and he pooped all over the floor," I tell Mr. Ed. "My mom was mad, but it was funny. It smelled and Peanuts wiped his butt across the carpet and left a brown mark."

"I had a dog when I was your age. His name was Smokey. He was a good dog. I'd always take him hunting with me."

"What did you hunt?"

"Deer, sometimes quail. You ever do any hunting?"

"No." I rock back and forth in the seat. "I love animals and don't want to kill them."

"But you eat animals, and somebody has to kill them."

"But I don't eat dogs and hamsters. I don't eat deer. I don't know what a quail is."

"A quail is a bird. A chicken is a bird, too. And someone kills those chickens that you eat."

"But don't their mommies get sad when they don't come home? I would be sad if somebody killed Josh to eat him."

I look at my food. I'm not hungry anymore. I close the box and put it on the floor. I miss Peanut and I miss Josh and I miss Mom. I wonder if they miss me. Sometimes they yell at me or tell me to hurry up and tie my shoes or walk fast or stop being gross. But I don't say that to them.

"Mr. Ed, can we call my mom now?"

"She said she was going call us. She had some things to take care of, but then she is going to call."

"Do you think she isn't going to call because she is mad at me?"

I feel tears in my eyes. Maybe I will never see Mom again and Mr. Ed will have to help me with my homework.

"I don't think so." He reaches over and pats me on the head. "You're taking a big-boy trip, huh?"

"Yeah, but I'm not a big boy. I'm fifteen. I'm not big enough to be on my own yet."

"I been on my own since I was sixteen." Mr. Ed laughs. He sounds like a cartoon man. Some people on the TV aren't real, like Yosemite Sam and Bugs Bunny and Transformers. But some people on TV are real. They're just acting. They are real on the TV and real not on TV, like Megan. There is a camera that takes pictures of people when they act and then the pictures are put in the TV. I'm not sure how they take pictures of cartoon characters since they are not real. I have to ask Josh when I get home.

"Did you become a truck driver when you grew up, Mr. Ed?" The big road looks different where we are than when we go to the beach. The trees are straight and don't have any arms reaching out. Which is good because sometimes the trees with arms scare me.

"I had a bunch of different jobs. Security guard. Bartender. Logger. But I've been driving trucks for fifteen years now."

"When I get bigger, I am going to be an army man or drive a truck."

"Drive a truck, Jimmy." Mr. Ed laughs again. "It's safer."

"Why?"

"Well, you could get killed if you're a soldier."

"But only bad guys die, Mr. Ed. The good guys kill them."

"Not always. Sometimes the good guys die, and the bad guys win."

"But that's not fair and I don't like it."

Mr. Ed hits me on the shoulder nice. I like Mr. Ed more than Dad because Dad yells at me. Dad doesn't hit me nice like Mr. Ed does.

"Don't worry. The good guys win a lot of the time."

"When Henry and I play army guys, we always win. Sometimes Henry is the bad guy and he make-believes dead. But he is not really dead. He's just pretending. Just like Megan pretends and Josh pretends. Only old people and bad people die. But not good people. Unless they are old."

Mr. Ed is quiet so I am quiet. We are on the big road. I count red cars and blue cars and black cars. They are small because they are far away but they are not really small. When we take trips on the big road, I count things. My mom told me to count things because it will make us go in the car faster.

But I don't know how long we are going to be on the big road. I don't know where Florida is. Mr. Ed says we will get there tonight, but I'm not sure how many hours there are until night is coming. I just hope that Mom calls soon so that I can tell her I'm okay and that Mr. Ed is taking care of me.

13.

I am counting cars and yellow lines on the road and trees and animals that were run over by other cars and big trucks and little cars. I don't want to be in the truck anymore. There is nothing to do in the truck but count and sing honky-tonk and eat lollipops.

My teeth feel slimy and I try to wipe it off with my tongue. It doesn't work so I rub my teeth with my sleeve. I want to walk around and play. But Mr. Ed does not stop. He keeps going and going. The dark is coming. My leg is sleeping.

"Mr. Ed, why hasn't Mom called?"

"I don't know." Mr. Ed doesn't look at me.

"I like the truck, but I don't want to be in the truck anymore. I want to go outside."

"Well, truckers are different. We have to drive as far as we can without making stops. Time is money for us. Sometimes I drive ten hours straight and I just pee in this container."

He pulls a big bottle from his side.

"Mr. Ed, that's just a bottle of lemonade."

He laughs, "You want to drink it?"

I open the bottle and smell it and it smells bad. Mr. Ed undoes himself and asks me for the bottle and I give it to him. He pees in it.

"Gotta go? I ain't stopping for a while."

He holds the bottle while I undo myself and then I put my pee-pee in the bottle and I pee it. My pee is in the bottle and so is Mr. Ed's pee but I can't tell my pee from his pee.

"I like undoing and going in the bottle," I laugh. "Can I take a bottle to my school and pee in class? I don't like to undo in school because the bathroom smells and sometimes there is poop on the floor and walls."

"The pee bottle is our secret. You like secrets?"

"I try but I'm not good at it. I will be better when I'm bigger."

"What do you mean, when you're bigger? You're a big boy, Jim. You're fifteen years old. You got a big-boy penis."

"You're *not* supposed to look at my pee-pee, Mr. Ed!"

"You want to know a secret?"

"Yes."

Mr. Ed pets his beard. "I don't know if I trust you."

"But I can. I *can* keep a secret!"

"Can you?"

"Lying is bad, Mr. Ed. God says so. If I lie to you, I will go to hell."

"Okay. The secret is that every man is always checking out every other man's pee-pee. They're always comparing, making sure theirs isn't too small."

Mr. Ed undoes himself again but he doesn't pee. He lets his pee-pee sit out and I laugh.

"See?" He smiles. "I think it's a pretty good-size pee-pee. Now, let's see yours again."

I undo and let my pee-pee sit out even though I am not peeing.

"See, Jimmy? You've got a big-boy pee-pee, too. But it's hard to tell how big it is until you get it hard. Have you ever gotten your pee-pee hard, Jimmy?"

"I don't know."

"Well, see, this is what you do."

He takes his pee-pee in his hand and pets it like I petted Mr. Kibble. Mr. Ed's pee-pee stands straight up.

"Now you do it."

I pet my pee-pee. Mom tells me not to touch my pee-pee when I am not peeing. But it feels good so I pet it some more. Then it gets big like Mr. Ed's. Mr. Ed makes a noise and he pees in the bottle but it is white.

"Why did you pee milk?"

"Milk is what comes out after your pee-pee gets hard. Here, make sure you get yours in the bottle."

I don't believe Mr. Ed. Because I am not a mommy and only a mommy can have milk for babies. But then it feels like I have to go really bad and I have to push my pee-pee down toward the bottle because it is still up. My pee comes out white, too.

"All right, buddy," Mr. Ed says when I hand the bottle back to him. "Now, if you need to pee or use the bottle for any reason, just let me know."

"Mr. Ed?"

"What is it?"

"Can I put my pee-pee back in now?"

14.

Mr. Ed says we are going to eat soon. But when Mom says we are going to eat soon we don't eat for awhile. I hope Mom and Josh have not forgotten about me. When we stop to eat, I will ask Mr. Ed if I can call Mom or maybe 911 so the police can come and get me. Maybe when I go home Mr. Ed can visit me but we will take a short ride, like to Megan's house or the toy store but not the big road. I like the big road but only when we go to the beach. Mr. Ed said we were going to the beach so maybe we are going tomorrow. We'll see, right?

The dark is coming. The last dark I was sleeping in Mr. Ed's truck but Mr. Ed has not been sleeping at all.

"Mr. Ed, how come you don't go to sleep?"

"Truckers' secret," he laughs.

Mr. Ed turns the radio up so he can hear the lady talk louder. Sometimes people talk on the radio. It's not just music. But the people who talk on the radio don't live in the radio. It is like TV, but you cannot see people on the radio. The lady is talking on the radio about a bad man. Somebody who killed a girl and ran away. Mr. Ed pushes the radio again and music comes out. A man is singing *Hey porter, Hey porter would you tell me the time.*

"Mr. Ed, I'm really hungry!"

My stomach hurts and I want to run and run and run. I don't like being in the truck. It is like being sick, except when I'm sick I sleep and don't get out of bed.

"All right, Jimmy. I heard you. You like McDonald's or Hardee's?"

"I want to eat scrambled eggs and sit at the big table."

"We don't got time to stop that long, Jimmy. We got to make it down to Florida."

The truck is slowing down and we are leaving the big road. There is a H-A-R-D-E-E'-S. Mr. Ed stops the truck using the stick on the floor. I put my hand on the door and push but it doesn't open.

"You stay here," Mr. Ed says.

He is holding his wallet.

"I'll go in and get us something."

"But Mr. Ed, I have to go potty!"

"All right. But we can't fool around. In and out, you understand?"

We are walking to the H-A-R-D-E-E'-S. There are other families walking in and out. They are going places too. I wonder if they are going to Florida. Inside the doorway there are little books with pictures of Mickey Mouse and crocodiles and water. I stop and pull out every one. I want Mom to help me cut out the pictures so I can paste them on my school folders.

Mr. Ed takes my hand to pull me into the restaurant. I pull away and I drop all my little books. Mom doesn't hold my hand. I tell Mr. Ed that I'm a big boy but he holds on and pushes my little books into the corner with his shoe. He goes in the toilet room with me. I sit down and undo and I am singing. *Hey porter, Hey porter would you tell me the time.* I have to go poop and it hurts a little. Mr. Ed is making a noise with his mouth like a bird. I can't remember the word. Josh can make the sound like the bird too.

I wash my hands with soap and water like I learned at school and then Mr. Ed takes my hand again and we walk to the front where you can pick food. I want the big sandwich on the wall and I want a chocolate shake. Mr. Ed tells the man our order and then they make the food.

Mr. Ed picks up the newspaper and looks through each part. Dad only looks through the paper with the football in it and Mom looks through the paper with people on TV in it. I like that paper because once Mom cut out a picture of Megan and taped it to my folder for school. Megan ripped and my Mom taped her together. Mr. Ed looks through all the papers and puts one paper in his arm.

I see a booth where I want to sit. There are a lot of people and I want to tell them about Big Thunder. But we don't eat inside. We go back to Big Thunder and we eat our food. Mr. Ed puts the newspaper under his seat.

I unwrap my sandwich and then make sure they didn't put pickles on it. "Why do we have to sit alone?"

"You just finish your dinner." Mr. Ed has meat coming out of his mouth. It moves when he chews.

I eat my sandwich and then my fries. I don't get sick. I take the straw out of the cup so I can get all of the shake out with my fingers. Sometimes I don't get all the shake out with the straw. Mom yells at me when I use my finger but Mr. Ed doesn't.

Mr. Ed balls his wrapper into a ball and puts it back in the bag. "Jimmy, I'm gonna hit the hay for a few hours. Why don't you come back here with me and take a nap?"

"But I want to talk to Mom."

I ball my wrapper up and I want to throw it outside.

"We'll call her after we take a nap."

"But I want to talk to Mom now!" I hold up my ball to throw at him.

"Well, son, we can't."

He holds out the bag for my wrapper. I want to throw it, but I don't. "I don't get a good signal on my cell phone here."

"But you said you were going to call! You lied!"

I slap the bag from his hand and I feel like I'm going to blow up.

"Blue!" I say.

"I didn't lie. It's not that we're not going to call your mom." Mr. Ed takes a pill out of his shirt pocket. "Now here, take this. It's a vitamin. You want to be a big, strong boy for the army, right?"

I don't have any shake to drink down the vitamin. Mr. Ed lets me have some of his soda.

"You just got to be patient." Mr. Ed reaches over and opens the door to the bed. "Now come and take a nap with me. I need to get some rest before we hit the final leg."

"What is that?"

"It means we're almost there!" Mr. Ed climbs into the bed. "And then we can go to the beach!"

I am excited that we are going to the beach. I can hold my breath under the water. I can hold it for a long time. I get in the bed next to Mr. Ed and hold my breath. 1, 2, 3, 4, 5, 6, 7, 8, 9, 10, 11, 12, 13, 14, 15, 16, 17, 18, 19, 20, 1, 2, 3, 4, 5, 6, 7, 8, 9, 10, 11, 12, 13, 14, 15, 16, 17, 18, 19, 20, 1, 2, 3, 4, 5, 6, 7, 8, 9, 10, 11, 12, 13, 14, 15, 16, 17, 18, 19, 20.

I am getting very sleepy. I close my eyes. I feel Mr. Ed's finger in my back. I reach my hand around my back to grab it away. I am worried he is going to tickle me but it is not Mr. Ed's finger it's his pee-pee. It is hard and sticking up like before. Mr. Ed holds my hand there as he undoes himself and he makes me touch it. It feels like mine except it is a little bigger and Mr. Ed has lots of hair around his. I have hair around mine but not as much as Mr. Ed does around his.

Mr. Ed keeps my hand on his pee-pee and undoes me with his other. He touches me like I'm touching him. It feels good. But Josh doesn't touch mine and Dad doesn't touch mine and Henry doesn't touch my mine and I do not touch theirs.

I feel good at first and then I pee milk and then I don't feel good. I am so tired and then it stops.

When I wake up Mr. Ed is snoring. My behind hurts so bad like when I go to the bathroom and have the runs. But it hurts more than that. It hurts so bad. Some people get sick from bad food. I get out of the bed and go to the front of the truck but I do it real quiet. I sit in Mr. Ed's seat and make-believe I am driving the truck. I turn the big wheel and say "honk honk!" but real quiet. There are many trucks beside Mr. Ed's truck and I think the men inside are sleeping, too.

Mr. Ed's wallet is on the dashboard. I pick it up and look at it. It's bigger than mine was. He has lots of cards like my mom and dad have that can buy you things if you do not have money but then you have to pay the money later. Mr. Ed also has a card like Josh and Mom and Dad that lets him drive. I look at the picture. It is Mr. Ed but he does not have a beard. And it says his name is J-O-N-A-T-H-A-N F-R-Y-E. I wonder why Mr. Ed calls himself Mr. Ed and not Mr. Jonathan. I want to ask him but he is still asleep.

I pick up the newspaper on the floor. I don't read very many words but I think the comics are funny. I look at the pictures and laugh.

I look through the newspaper and I am happy because there is a picture of me in it! It says police are S-E-A-R-C-H-I-N-G for boy wanted in C-O-N-N-E-C-T-I-O-N with girl's M-U-R-D-E-R. And my name, Jimmy Dembrowski, is under the picture! I wonder why Mr. Ed or Mr. Jonathan did not tell me about my picture in the paper. When my picture was in the paper from the Special Olympics, Mom put the picture on our refrigerator and also when I won the Halloween contest at the mall. I was a GI Joe.

I put the newspaper in my backpack because when I get home Mom will want to put the picture up even though it's only my school picture that is in the newspaper and not a new picture. I look through the windshield and I see a telephone. I can call Mom while Mr. Ed or Mr. Jonathan is sleeping and let her know that I'm okay, that we're almost to Florida, and then we're going to the beach.

15.

I climb out of the truck and walk to the restaurant. My butt still hurts bad. Maybe if I get toilet paper and put it in my pants I won't hurt so much. In the bathroom I sit down and undo and there is blood all on my underpants. I am scared that I will die because I am bleeding. I stuff my behind with toilet paper so I don't die. I am still very sleepy and almost fall off the toilet.

"My butt is bleeding," I tell the lady at the counter. "I think I'm dying."

"Do you want me to call an ambulance?" she asks.

"Can you call my mom instead?"

But I don't know my number so she calls 911. She gives me a small Coke with ice and tells me to sit in the booth. I tell her I need to tell Mr. Ed that the police are taking me home and I walk outside with the Coke.

I wonder if Mr. Ed's behind hurts, too. I am on my way to the truck when I see him climbing out.

"Mr. Ed," I say when he gets to me. "My butt is bleeding."

Mr. Ed grabs my arm and is pulling me back to the truck. "We got to get back on the road."

"But the lady at the restaurant called 911 because my butt hurts." We are walking toward the truck but Mr. Ed is walking faster than me. I feel like I am going to fall down because I can't make my legs move like they are supposed to.

Mr. Ed is grabbing my arm so hard it is hurting. I start to cry. "Be quiet, Jimmy. All the good things I've done for you, and then you can't even listen. Why can't you listen when an adult talks to you?"

"But Mr. Ed, your name on the card says J-O-N-A-T-H-A-N F-R-Y-E."

Mr. Ed opens the door on my side. "Get in. First of all, you're not supposed to go through things that aren't yours. Second, my own mother calls me Ed. So do my friends."

"But the lady on the phone told me to wait and the police would pick me up," I say, when Mr. Ed climbs in on the other side.

"You want to get arrested, Jimmy? You want me to get arrested for harboring a criminal?"

I do not understand Mr. Ed's words but I am sad because I am not going home. I am a big boy and Dad told me not to cry but I am crying.

"You killed that girl, Jimmy." Mr Ed says. "You want to go to jail?"

"I did not kill anybody, Mr. Ed."

"You killed that girl. There's a manhunt after you. If I were smart, I'd have left you right where you were so the police would have arrested you."

"I didn't do anything and I didn't kill anybody! I just want to go home!"

"Jimmy, if you go home you're in big trouble. I've been trying to keep you from getting in trouble. But if I take you home, I'm going to get in trouble too. Do you want Mr. Ed to go to jail?"

"I can keep a secret!"

"Believe me, you will," Mr. Ed says. He looks like Dad when he is about to punish me. I do not like Mr. Ed or Mr. J-O-N-A-T-H-A-N F-R-Y-E anymore. I try to open the door to jump out of the truck like on the television but it won't open.

"Mr. Ed, I'm sorry."

I tug at his arm. "I'll be good! I swear!"

"Just fucking shut up." Mr. Ed hits me on the side of the head and I see little lights.

"Blue!"

He hits me again even when I cannot see him. I reach far and put my hands on his neck. His neck is big and scratchy, not like Megan's. He puts his hands on my hands and the truck moves very hard but the wrong way. I go into my side of the truck, against the window. The other cars are honking. Mr. Ed makes the truck move the right way by turning on the wheel. Then he reaches under the seat and he comes up with a gun. He points it at me.

"Get in the back and shut the hell up before I blow your fucking head off," he says. "I shoulda done that a long time ago."

If he shoots me it might be make-believe, but I don't know.

I get in the back of the truck and sit on the bed. Mr. Ed is a bad guy but he does not look like one. How can you tell that a bad guy is bad if he looks good?

He is going to hurt me. I am crying and my eyes feel big and my nose feels big and my chest feels big and my stomach feels big. I want my mom to blow on me to make the hurt stop but I don't think she can blow all over me enough.

I wonder if I will be dead. If I am a ghost I can go to school but people won't see me. And that will make me sad. But I am not dead now. Megan is just make-believe dead. If you just hit someone they will not die. You have to shoot them with a gun or hit them with an arrow like an Indian. Like Tonto and the Lone Ranger.

But I still worry I will be dead. Sometimes things die that aren't bad. My fish died and he was not old or bad. Maybe good people die, too.

I wish I didn't go to California before dinner.

It is dark. When I am in trouble, Mom sends me to our room but it is not dark and I can play with my toys if I'm really quiet. I put my hand in front of my face but I can see it only a little.

Tomorrow it is Friday and I have school. I wonder if Mrs. Rawlings misses me. I bet she thinks I have the flu.

Sometimes I do not go to school because my tummy hurts and I'm hot. I have to stay home because I have germs and if other people get my germs, they will get sick too. I asked Mom how other people will get my germs and she said you touch other people and you can give them your germs. She said they are very small so I can't see them. But sometimes I look at my hands and I can see them. I showed them to Josh and he said the brown germs were just dirt. I wonder if I touch Mr. Ed if I can give him some germs to make him sick. If he kills me maybe I can be a ghost and scare him.

I look out the little window above the bed. I can see the cars on their sides from this window, not the front and back. It is still the big road though. It's like when I sit in the backseat when I ride with Mom and Dad. I can see other people in the cars. I don't know if they see me. I see a little doggie in one of the cars. His head is out the window and the window is blowing his fur. Once I put my head out the window and the wind hurt and Dad yelled at me. The little doggie has his head out of the window. I am scared the wind is hurting him.

"Little doggie!" I yell. "Get in the car! Get in!"

I hit the window with my fist but he cannot hear me. But the lady in Mom's seat sees me. I wave at her from the window and I point at her little doggie because I am worried. She looks at me but she doesn't smile. She is pointing at me and talking to the person driving the car and she is pointing at me. I wave and I yell my name and she is making a call on her phone. She could be calling Mr. Ed, but he says his phone doesn't get reception so maybe she is calling someone else. I hope it is my mom.

The little doggie puts his head back in the window, but the lady is still looking at me. I pull the newspaper out of my bag. I can't see my picture in the dark, but I want to show the lady that I am in the newspaper. I put the newspaper with my picture against the glass so she can see. This is the third time my picture is in the newspaper. I am famous like the Batman.

16.

I say my prayers like I do every night. I pray for Mom and Dad and Josh and Mrs. Rawlings and Henry and the girl in the wheelchair. Mr. Ed is a bad guy but I pray for him because I would not be a good guy if I did not.

I pray for me too.

The truck is stopping. I wonder if we are in Florida. I wonder if I could see Disneyworld if I were in the front with Mr. Ed. If I wave really hard maybe Buzz Lightyear will see me and wave back. I look out the window. It is dark but I can see the police car lights. The door to me opens and a policeman helps me out.

"You got my 911!" I say to him.

"We've gotten a few calls about you, Jimmy," he says.

When I get out of the truck Mr. Ed is wearing handcuffs like a bad guy. He looks mad at me.

"Why are you arresting me?" he says to the policeman. "Is it illegal to pick up a hitchhiker? Tell him, Jimmy. I was just giving you a ride."

"He hit me!" I yell. "He has a gun!"

I wonder if Mr. Ed will get in trouble. I wonder if I can have Mr. Ed's gun if he goes to jail so I can kill other bad guys. I get to ride in a police car to the police station but not the police car that Mr. Ed is in. On the way to the police station, the police ask me if I'm hungry and I say that I ate dinner but could we stop for a shake? The police man laughs and I ask again but we do not get a shake. In the police car there is a wire between where the police sit and where I sit. Our car doesn't have wire but when we take Peanut to the doctor that animals go to there are lots of wire boxes where animals sleep.

"Is my mom coming?" I ask the policeman in Dad's seat.

"Your family will be here tomorrow," he says.

"We'll be keeping you at the police station tonight."

I am happy because I will be at the police station, where the good guys are. Once at school we did a field trip and we got fingerprinted and we saw where the bad guys go.

"I've been to the police station before," I say to the policeman in Mom's seat.

"Well, that's a good thing," he laughs.

I don't know why it's funny, but I laugh too.

There are lots of policemen in the police station. I wave to them and they wave back. I ask if I can see the police doggies and they say that they are out doing police work.

"Maybe later, right?" I ask but nobody answers.

I see lots of bad guys in handcuffs. The police take my backpack and touch my pockets and all over me. They take my picture and make my fingerprints. On the field trip I took with my school they gave us our fingerprints back. One boy in my class was crying because they took his fingerprints, but Mrs. Rawlings told us they weren't really taking our fingerprints, they were just making copies of them.

I ask the policeman if I can have my fingerprints back and

he says no. I ask if I can have my army men and the policeman tells me I can have them later. I don't like this police station very much. The policemen aren't as nice as at our police station.

I sit in a room. There are no windows but there is a mirror and I try to comb my hair with my fingers because Mom will be mad that I am dirty. The police lady brings me a Coke. I ask for a cup with ice. The police lady brings back a cup with ice and some coloring books. I color for awhile but I want to see Mom and Josh. The police lady says I can't see them until tomorrow. I ask her if I can see her gun and she laughs. She tells me to come with her and we walk down the hall and to the place where the bad guys are kept.

"You try and get some sleep," the police lady says, opening one of the bad guy rooms with the bars. "Your family will be here and then we're going to ask you some questions, okay?"

I stand in front of the room but do not go in.

"I don't want to sleep here. I didn't do anything! I'll be good!"

"It's just for the night, Jimmy," the police lady says and pats me on the shoulder. "These are the only beds we have in the police station. It's okay. You're tired, aren't you?"

I nod and the police lady closes the bars. I would rather be in Mr. Ed's truck than be here. I want my army men and I want my backpack and I really want Mr. Ed's lollipops. I forgot to take them from the truck.

I am by myself and it is dark. But I am a big boy and I am going home tomorrow and it will be over.

I squeeze my eyes and say I am an army man.

I am a good guy.

I am an army man.

I am a good guy.

Tomorrow I will go home and everything will be the way it used to be before I went to California.

17.

I wake up and it is Saturday. I don't have school and I am confused but then I remember that I am at the police station. Another police man comes and gets me and I go to wash. I ask him to help me with the shower because it is not the shower at my house. He turns the knobs and asks me if the shower is too hot.

"It's good," I answer. "Don't worry, you can look at it."

"Look at what?" he asks.

"You can look at my pee-pee," I explain. "I know all men look at other men's pee-pees to see if they are big boys. It's our secret."

The man looks at me like he smells a fart and leaves. I rub my arms and my legs and my back and my stomach and my hair with soap and I pet it. It is bad to touch it and I shouldn't but it feels good. I pet it and pet it and I pee milk but then I feel bad. I want to unhear what Mr. Ed says to me because now I am blowing up all the time.

"Blue! Blue! Blue!" I say. A policeman comes back but it is a different one. He asks me if I'm okay. I ask him if he wants to see it and he tells me to get dressed.

"I'm not a fag," I tell him.

I dry my legs and my arms and my back and my stomach and my hair but I leave it wet. I am afraid to touch it even though I feel like I will blow up. My butt isn't bleeding anymore but it still hurts bad.

I put my old clothes back on because I do not have new clothes to wear. Even my underpants with blood on them. I stuff more toilet paper in them. But maybe Mom will bring me clothes from home like when we take clothes on vacation. I hope she packed my Baltimore Orioles shirt. I like to wear it at the beach and when we go to baseball games and on Saturdays. I am wearing my Wednesday shirt. It is green and has stripes. I ask the policeman if I can have my backpack and my army men and he says later.

I am so happy when Mom and Dad and Josh come. Mom hugs me and she is crying and I am crying but I am happy.

"Jimmy, thank God you're okay," Mom says. She puts her hands on both sides of my face and she kisses my forehead. "We missed you so much. We love you so much. You know how much we love you, right?" She makes my eyes meet her eyes, like when she makes me promise to do something.

I hug her. I have not smelled anything like Mom in lots of days. All the things I remember about Mom and Dad and Josh I am thinking about. Soon I will be home and I won't have to remember them anymore because they will be there.

A man comes and talks to Mom and Dad and then me. He is not wearing a police suit so I know he is not a policeman. He says he is a detective and that he is going to ask me questions but it is not a test. There are no right answers, he says—I only have to tell the truth. There is also a man who is a lawyer. His name is Mr. Reed and he says he will help me answer the questions.

I ask him if it's cheating and he says it's not. I wonder if Mrs. Rawlings will let Mr. Reed help me with my adding test.

I tell the detective and Mr. Reed everything that happened. Mr. Reed asks me if I understand how people die. The detective and Mr. Reed write a lot on their pads. I want a pad so I can write, too, but then the detective gives me my backpack and GI Joes and newspaper back.

Mom and Dad and Josh are outside the room. Mom hugs me and she is crying and I am crying. Mom and Dad go in the room with the detective and Mr. Reed. They give me and Josh a basketball and let us play on the court behind the police station. The police station is a lot like school. You take tests and have recess and they feed you but you are being punished.

"When are we going home?"

I throw the basketball toward the basket but miss everything. The ball rolls away toward the fence.

"I don't know, Jimmy." Josh runs after the ball and then he dribbles it back. I run toward him but he shoots before I get there and makes a basket.

I am holding the ball against my stomach.

"I'm tired of being here."

"Jimmy, that girl is dead and everybody thinks you did it." Josh knocks the ball out of my hands and goes toward the basket. I run after him, swatting at his arms.

"But Megan is not dead. She is on the TV," I say. Josh turns away from me and he dribbles. Pat-pat-pat.

"That girl is *dead*, Jimmy."

"No, she's not. You're lying!"

"Stop it."

Josh shoots and misses. I take the ball and run down to the other basket because I don't like the game he is playing. I think he is kidding and we will go home and have pizza. But I am not sure. Josh sits down at the other end of the court. I throw the ball at him. He grabs it with both hands and throws it hard back at me.

"Josh, why are you crying?" He doesn't look at me. Sometimes people cry when they're happy and some people cry when they're sad. Sometimes people cry when they're scared and some people cry when they're angry. "I'm sorry I got you in trouble."

"It's okay. You're a good brother."

He puts his arms around his knees and rocks on the ground. The only time Josh was crying was when his girlfriend broke up with him. But then they got back together and he stopped. I kick him in the side with my foot. But nice.

He does not move so I pat him on the shoulder and he gets up. He wipes his face on his shirt.

"All right, Jimmy, three-pointer time."

Josh points toward the basket. "All net, okay?"

I back up and run a couple of steps and throw the basketball as hard as I can. The basketball goes over the backboard and over the fence and into the parking lot.

"Wait, Jimmy, I'll get it," Josh says.

But I am already running out of the basketball court and into parking lot after the ball. There is a policeman running toward me yelling. I think I have gone too far. I put my hands up, like a bad guy.

The ball keeps rolling. It rolls out in the street. And a police car comes in from another road and runs it over. It makes a loud sound, like a gunshot on TV and I am scared a little. I look back at Josh. He looks scared, too, but then it is funny, like a big fart. We laugh.

MAY-SEPTEMBER

1.

Alice would come shortly. Sandra waited in the breakfast room, wiping her fingerprints off the laptop, her crumbs off the table. She had chosen slacks because it was not quite warm yet and her legs were pale, freckled with brown.

The blog was Andrea's idea. A blog for Beatrice and Elvin to read about their grandmother before she grew cotton for brains and peed her pants. No, she did not have Alzheimer's, she would assure Alice. But she was at the age where anything could happen. Jack was not at that age and it had already happened, and it had happened to many of her acquaintances already. One must be prepared.

The memoir pleased her. She had always written, she would tell Alice, here and there when Andrea was born and Jack was still alive.

The blog did not. An idea from a magazine, surely—her daughter's entire life was molded by *Women's Day* and *Better Homes and Gardens*. How to baste a turkey. How to have better sex. How to not feel guilty about being a failure.

She had not been the best mother. But she went to the store and she bought a computer and some young man came who looked at her shoulders, not her face, and set it up in the breakfast room of her condo, where there was a lot of light and where it was far enough from the Steinway that she wouldn't scoot over and start tapping on the keys instead of the keyboard.

She sat at the table, the laptop humming quietly, nonjudgmental, waiting for the contents of her labor. Beside it sat the yellow-lined notepad filled with her thoughts. A scroll blue and small and wound so tight it could break.

Andrea had tried to talk her through the process on the phone—setting up the account, adding pictures, typing entries and labeling them and organizing archives. She said yes, yes, yes, all the while knowing she would never remember these things. She wished she would die and leave the grandchildren nothing but her money, no stories, no strings. And when she hung up with Andrea, full of assurances that her first post would be forthcoming in hours, days, oh, but soon, she turned away from the friendly little void and played some of Chopin's etudes, the notes coughing out of her fingers.

Alice would hear her playing the Chopin and be comforted by Sandra's stature. She imagined Alice would be relieved she was not some crazy widow whose house smelled like coffee and rot. She had posted the ad at the bookstore, the coffee shop. Once a week—help writing memoirs on computer. Handsome reimbursement. It sounded weak, desperate. A few calls came. A veteran of World War II, a contemporary of her father almost, who had even less computer experience than she. A female science fiction enthusiast and part-time Wiccan. And then Alice.

Alice was young. Her voice was a smooth, melodic voice on the phone, slightly upturned, inquisitive. Insincere. But eager for handsome reimbursement. Alice was working at a bookstore, had an MFA. She would love to help with editing, ghostwriting, humoring an old woman at nine o'clock on Saturday mornings. Yes, she specified the time. Nine o'clock. She didn't want some young woman who went out on Friday nights, someone who wouldn't take her seriously.

Sandra had written two pages but Alice would not be judgmental. A friendly little void, transcribing the contents of her labor. Sandra would play a little Barber, Beethoven, and explain how she had dreamed of being a concert pianist. Alice would understand dreams. Not like Andrea, who never wanted to hear. Alice, hungry for handsome reimbursement, would like music.

Sandra had made a pot of coffee but thought better of it and boiled water for tea, too. She wondered whether she should have worn a skirt.

The rap at the door was soft, hesitant. Not hesitant for handsome reward, perhaps, but for the contents of her labor. But she needed Alice; surely Alice knew that. She was at the age where anything could happen.

Sandra opened the door.

Mrs. Holiday? The girl straightened her glasses with her thumb and forefinger. I'm Alice.

2.

Sandra, please. She held out her hand to Alice. Come in.

Alice ran her fingers through her hair, long, brown, her eyes studying the apartment. A splash of lilies on the table, cinnamon and violet and butter ones, bled into the reflection of window rain beneath them. The rain bled on the Steinway in the corner shadow and the coffee table and the low-light glass frames on the walls and the grandfather clock and Alice wondered how someone could live in a room full of rain.

Would you like something to drink? Sandra moved toward the kitchen. I'm having a coffee. But I also have tea. Please don't be polite and say you're not thirsty.

Tea's fine. Alice looked for a place to drop her bag but felt that the room would repel it, the walls, the furniture slippery with rain. And Sandra, with streaks of rain down her face. Deep riverbeds from cheek to chin. Eyes full of water and blue. Whites so watery that the blues might float away. Silver waves of hair, short, undulating, brushed away from her face.

You have a beautiful home.

I moved here ten years ago when my husband died. Sandra's eyes measured the water from the teapot into a mug. What would you like? I've got lemon zinger and Earl Grey.

Lemon zinger. Alice dipped the teabag into the water. I'm sorry about your husband.

Everyone dies. Sandra poured coffee, black, into a mug. Alice watched the bones of Sandra's elbows poke at the yolk of her brown turtleneck sweater, her small hips swaddled in her sandy linen slacks.

So. Alice sipped at the water infused with herbs, her tongue afloat in the room of water. She coughed. You want to blog your memoirs?

Yes, my daughter's idea. Sandra sat in front of the computer, to the left of Alice. She suggested I write them so my grandchildren can enjoy them. They live far away, in Florida. I see them once or twice a year.

Alice nodded. It won't be any trouble to get you up and running.

My grandchildren won't find my life interesting. And I'm sure you won't, either. Sandra sipped at her coffee. But I will pay you well for very little.

Alice filled her mouth with tea. Sandra looked at her, her water and blue eyes moving around Alice's face and into her own eyes and then her soft mouth. Alice swallowed. She had taught continuing education classes for a time after grad school, found the older adults eager but bashful. Overwhelmed by expression and its evolving modes. They thanked her like immigrants, touching her forearm, bringing her cookies.

You are afraid to ask, so I will tell you. I think thirty dollars an hour is fair. We can meet Saturday mornings at nine. We can get started today. I've already written some things down. Sandra pushed the notepad toward Alice.

Have you set up the blog yet? Alice looked at the writing, then at Sandra's hands, white and growing twisted over the coffee mug.

No. Sandra pushed the new laptop toward Alice. That will be your job.

Alice settled the laptop into her hands. Her own children lived as words in computers, in happy blank boxes like this one. She nursed the baby, waking it up, feeding it with her fingers, and it cooed and purred and a bright happy blog was born. Alice filled her mouth with tea to quench the dry. Outside, it drizzled.

Are you unwell? Sandra's brow wrinkled.

I have a little cough. Alice turned the computer screen toward Sandra. How do you like what I've done so far?

It's very professional. Sandra nodded, and the wrinkles in her head melted away and she smiled a little. Did you learn this at school?

No. Alice shook her head. Anyone can do this. I'll show you. You were born in 1940, your notes say?

Yes. My father volunteered for the war and was sent off to Guadalcanal in '42, leaving a wife and two children behind. He probably liked that better than being at home. He was killed, and we were destitute. I had two dresses for school. We had no heat and my sister and I slept in the bed with my mother. But this will all be in the memoirs—you don't need to be bored twice.

Perhaps I'm overstepping my bounds. Alice looked at Sandra's. But I will find it hard to work on this project if you are always so gruff.

Sandra's eyes widened, blinked. Alice's hands let go of the laptop, felt the floor with her feet.

I'm sorry. Alice shook her head, her face hot. What I meant was, well, every story is meaningful, and for you to denigrate…

Don't apologize. Sandra's hand unfurled from the coffee cup and touched Alice's arm. You're absolutely right. I don't have guests often. I forget my manners.

Sandra stood and swept away the coffee cups, clang-clang, into the sink.

The boy who set this up didn't even look at me. Sandra returned, pushed the laptop, almost too heavy for her hands, into a black leather case. Age makes one invisible. I do not harbor hopes that my memoirs will change this.

Alice clutched her bag. She wondered whether she had enough money for the bus, whether Sandra would pay her by cash or check. Whether she would pay today. Whether she would pay at all.

You look at me. Sandra bent her head toward the living room. That's something. Come. I'll play for you before you go.

3.

When Alice came Sandra made tea and served petit fours from the bakery downtown. She served pink and white petit fours in 1968 when she had Jack's colleagues' wives over for tea and bridge. Andrea would eat the walls of icing off, leave spongy yellow innards on her play table and blame it on her dolls. She served mint green and chocolate ones in 1972 during Nixon's inauguration. Jack smoked a cigar and the ashes burned a hole in the carpet. And pink and white in 1986 during Andrea's baby shower for Beatrice. Yellow and chocolate for when Alice came.

When Alice came, Sandra put out fresh flowers. When Jack died and she moved to the condo, she made tea and served petit fours, bought fresh flowers for visitors. She played Schubert and Mozart for Patricia and Donald and when Donald died she played Gershwin for Patricia. She played Beethoven and Grieg for Jean and Stuart and when they moved to Florida she played Grieg for Anna. When Anna couldn't come anymore she didn't play Grieg, either.

When Alice came, Sandra asked what she wanted her to play and Alice said she didn't care so Sandra played a little Grieg but Sandra seemed to like Beethoven so she played Beethoven.

Jack was a chemist—he developed household products. Sandra told Alice, drinking her coffee. She could not eat the petit fours now because of the sugar. He patented a chemical that made nail polish dry faster. Of course, he patented other chemicals, but I daresay that was the one we lived the most comfortably from. I wasn't attracted to Jack, but my family was incredibly poor. I thought I'd become a concert pianist, although I didn't know exactly how one became one, with my meager resources. We didn't have a piano at home growing up, but I was always fascinated by the piano at school. The music teacher, Mr. Stanley, gave me lessons, provided I did chores for Mrs. Stanley. She was a sickly woman who stayed in bed a lot. She's what we'd call bipolar today. But I was quite good.

So what happened? Alice looked up from the laptop. Sandra's words reflected in her curved glasses. Her hair curled onto her plump cheeks, baby bottoms.

I married Jack. I met him at some mixer at school. He was heading to college, and there I was, ready to go to secretary school. There was a very small chance I'd become a concert pianist. When Jack came around still, after I graduated high school, my mother practically proposed for him. I had wanted to take my chances. I was used to being incredibly poor. Now I'm used to being comfortably rich, and I guess not everyone can say that.

We should upload some pictures—do you have any pictures I could take home and scan?

I don't look at my pictures anymore. I'll have to give them to you next week, unless you want to come pick them up earlier— you'd be reimbursed for coming.

Well, why don't you see what you find. Alice picked up a petit four. And then we'll decide when I can get them.

You're busy—I understand. I suppose it's different these days, women with their careers, lives. Women don't marry for security now. Do they marry for love?

I don't know. Alice shook her head, put the petit four back on her plate.

I suppose when the right man comes along. My Andrea said she'd never get married. If marriage is so loveless like yours, she'd always cry to me, I don't want any part of it. But the right man comes along sometimes. You'll see.

I'm a lesbian. Alice looked at Sandra.

Oh. Sandra stood up and refilled her coffee. More tea? She smiled; her heart leaped a little. Jack hadn't known her. He knew her in a way, and she had his daughter, but he hadn't actually known her. And, she supposed, she hadn't known him. Although she had tried. Jack lived in his equations, his laboratory notebooks. He sat in his office, his head low, his hand moving along the notebooks. A pencil transformed his thoughts into lead equations, a ticking clock scratching pencil metronome. She could keep time to Jack, play along with him. Mozart, always.

You know, you don't have to do all this. Alice motioned to the petit fours. I mean, I enjoy it, but I'm hardly worth the effort.

Please. I don't have many visitors, and I've always enjoyed entertaining. White and red and green petit fours, 1967, Christmas Eve "Holiday" party. They had the party at their house every year to play off the joke of their name. Sandra played "Have Yourself a Merry Little Christmas" on the piano while Jack's colleague Leroy hung the mistletoe over her head and kissed her neck. She felt his lips through her shoulder, her elbows, her fingers, and she missed a note and everyone laughed and she started over. And Sandra and Leroy started.

Have you always dated women? Sandra looked at her hands. We didn't know many gay people. It wasn't something that people were open about back in the day.

Yes, mostly I've dated women. But I'd prefer... I hate to answer questions like this because it implies that it's a choice or that there's uncertainty involved on my part. For instance, people never ask you if you've only loved men.

No, I suppose they don't. Forgive me. I'm an old woman. I don't always know what's polite.

You don't have to apologize for being curious. And you certainly don't have to apologize for being sixty-seven. You're not old at all.

When you're sixty-seven, you let me know if you feel old. Sandra laughed. Jack ate meat, smoked. They all did. They all smoked so much back then. And drank. Gimlets, rye, martinis. Only the Christians didn't drink, only on Sundays. They all ate meat and potatoes and smoked and it was no surprise, the doctors said. High cholesterol, risk for heart attack, stroke. Jack took the pills and walked on the treadmill and they quit smoking and started drinking carrot juice and didn't laugh as loudly but what was the point if you couldn't. They no longer ate petit fours, white and pink and yellow and green at bridge, no longer smoked and drank gimlets. And Jack still died. But everyone does. She shouldn't have been, she thought, so surprised.

I dated some men in college. Alice took off her glasses, studied the frames. Sandra's words disappeared from Alice's face and Alice's green eyes Sandra saw. I lived with a woman for five years.

At least you had that. I mean, a love that long. Sometimes you're never even in love to begin with. Sandra reached for the plate. Please, take these with you. I can't have them anymore, and I'd hate for them to go to waste.

Alice took the petit-fours. Sandra dabbed the crumbs off Alice's plate with her finger, touched them to her tongue. She thought about when she and Leroy started. He mixed the martinis at the Christmas party because Jack made a lousy one. Leroy shook her martini in the silver bullet and the clear alcohol streamed out into her glass, her fingers on the stem. Leroy's pinky brushed the top of her palm as he rinsed out the bullet. He winked. Leroy made Sandra three martinis and then had her on top of the washer. She took her time getting back to the party in case Jack kept track of her comings and goings. She stopped and said goodnight to Andrea, took her little face in her big hands and brought it close. Andrea blinked and smiled, asked if Santa had come. He hasn't come, Sandra said, stroking her little face, not until everyone is asleep. Andrea asked for Sandra to bring her a petit four, and Sandra said of course, darling. But when she went back to the party, she stood opposite of Leroy, and his eyes, gray and bloodshot, she saw. She forgot.

4.

The photos were black and white, color bright, and faded. Torn edges, pin holes in corners, cigarette smelling, coffee splattered. Children in jumpers clutching dolls. A man with horn-rimmed glasses reading a book. The same man and Sandra standing in front of a jaguar convertible in a driveway, his fingers curling around her waist. A different man with gray eyes, blond hair, a scar on his chin. Birthday cakes. Collies on green lawns cropped flat like carpet. Sandra spread them over the table chronologically. Grade school, Sandra's teeth as large as her eyes. Her high school graduation in 1958. Her marriage in 1960. Andrea's birth in 1963. Sandra at the piano, various years, her hair long, blond, then bobbed, then cropped close to her skull. As it was now. From left to right her smooth face grew lines, spots. Her neck collapsed in her chest. She shrunk. Veins grew out of her wrists, hands. Andrea grew larger, long bones, pointy chin, smirking, leaning against Sandra. Sandra with the same smile always, always slightly pained. Or maybe the pain was in the eyes, cloaked and wet, the thing hidden from sight. Alice could not tell.

I was playing Schumann there. Sandra touched the photo that Alice held in her hand.

How do you know? Alice put the photo down, picked up another. What about this one?

Beethoven's Sonata No. 14. Sandra let her palm hover above the photos. I remember because I loved music more than my life. That sounds so dramatic, but it's true. Please don't put that in the blog.

Alice laughed. She put her hand over her mouth. I'm sorry. I shouldn't laugh. You just surprise me, the things you say.

It's not totally true. I loved Jack, and Jack loved me. In our own ways. We both adored Andrea. I love my grandchildren, spoiled and incurious as they are. But music is an unconditional love. Unconditional in what it gives to you. Am I wrong in thinking writing is the same?

I never thought of it as something good or bad or redemptive, Alice shrugged. With the money from her first paycheck, she had brought grapes, melons, plain yogurt, pecans, for Sandra, wrapped in cellophane from the market. The paper lay open on the table, catching light kaleidoscope, the ribbon, cranberry colored, unfurled on the table glass. I never thought of it as anything except as something that was a part of me, like breathing.

Sandra picked a grape off the stem, so bulbous and waxy. She held it like a coin. If my questions aren't too intrusive, what do you write about?

Alice wrote about relationships and heartbreak and people who were unsatisfied and disaffected but whose dissatisfaction and disaffection seemed somehow larger, more momentous than other people's. She wrote about parents dying, lovers dying, pets dying, dreams dying, seasons dying, night dying, day dying. And sometimes children were born and sometimes dreams were born and days were born and certainly nights. Sometimes love was born. Alice wrote about all the things that everyone wrote about and she didn't know why hers would be any better or different but she knew it didn't matter because she could never stop. When she got home she was going to write about the bulbous and waxy grape in Sandra's fingers. Alice would write that Sandra put it in her mouth and felt it with her tongue but did not break the skin, taste the juice.

You can read some if you'd like. Alice was writing a story about her ex only it wasn't her ex. Her ex worked at the university library; the ex in her story was a veterinarian. But they both felt stuck in their relationship with Alice, who was not Alice in the story. But Alice didn't know why either ex felt stuck, why their love stopped. Or why hers had continued.

You bring a story next time. Sandra brought the grape to her lips. And I'll certainly read it.

I'll have these up on the website tomorrow. Alice put the photos in her bag. If Alice had brought photos they would be of her parents in Wilkes Barre, Pennsylvania. A picture of her Girl Scout troop. A picture of her at the Y, her hair tucked under a pink rubber cap. Alice at fifteen with her mother after Alice's father died of lung cancer. Her mother had died then, too, but she was still living, her hands moving in dough, those hands white with the flour of the tarts and pies and bread pudding being born from them.

If Alice brought photos she would bring a photo of her ex, Lauren, the picture in front of the Grand Canyon. They had never seen a hole so big, one that could swallow them so fully and no one would know it. They held each other in front of the hole and a man from Kentucky took the picture. They smiled. Their cheeks and noses were pink. The sun bounced off their sunglasses. Nothing as big as that hole could come between them, they knew then. They could see a hole like that coming from a mile away, surely. Unless they were in the hole. It was possible that they were in the hole already when they met. But who had gotten out of the hole and who stayed, Alice was not sure.

If Alice brought photos they would be pictures that had not yet been taken. A picture of her and Lauren back together in front of Niagara Falls. A picture of Alice's mother in front of her own bakery. A picture of Alice and her father planting cucumbers, peppers, tomatoes, in the garden patch behind Alice's apartment. A picture of an adopted baby in Alice's arms, Lauren grabbing one little foot, her other hand curling around Alice's waist.

Is everything all right?

Yes. Alice shook her head. Everything is fine.

Do you have time to stay awhile? I'll reimburse you.

I could stay for a little while. Alice nodded. She did not want to go home just yet, where there were pictures of Lauren and some of her things. A pair of hiking boots with a rip in the toe. Some books they had shared, CDs. Memories that still breathed the air of her apartment, although she could not see them. Even the sweater she was wearing, a caramel-colored cashmere Lauren had given her for her birthday, pulled on her, itched her with memory.

Are you going to play something?

5.

Not just now, unless you want me to. Sandra fingered the scarf on her neck. Since Alice had come to visit, Sandra had worn a purple, a yellow, a paisley scarf. She did not like her sagging neck, the hollow between her collar bones. Would you like me to play something?

In the living room Sandra found the sheet music, Concerto in F by Gershwin. For years she had known most music by heart, but the last few years a note would fall out here, there, and she could not find it, would stop playing and begin again, only to drop a note someplace else. She began to forget entire songs altogether. Sometimes she could not reach quickly enough to the high notes or the lower notes, and her soles hurt when she pressed on the foot pedals. She had had enemies in her life, surely everyone did. But she hadn't expected her hands or her piano to turn against her.

When she and Leroy ended, she had not expected it, either. She had expected to leave Jack, to move into Leroy's Tudor across town. Leroy's wife had just moved out. In Sandra and

Jack's guestroom Leroy stroked her earlobe, reached across her on the bed to pull a cigarette from his pack. Don't get me wrong, Sandy. I'm glad she's gone. I just wish she hadn't taken the girls. But at least there will be room for you and Andrea.

Leroy's wife blinked too much, looked too long, took things too far. Sandra and Jack always made a little bet before parties as to how many drinks it would take before Leroy's wife went loopy. In the guest room Leroy pulled on his pants. Jack would be home soon. Sandra always remembered to empty the trash with the condom, the ashtray with Leroy's cigarettes. Then Andrea would come home from school and Sandra let her have a Bergers cookie and they would sit on the piano bench and Sandra would play.

Alice stood by the piano and Sandra patted the seat. Here, sit, like my daughter used to. She opened the sheet music, felt Alice's weight on the bench. My daughter has no aptitude for music. None for chemistry, either. Go figure. Lazy and spoiled. Like Leroy, she thought. She could almost swear Andrea was Leroy's child. But Leroy's child was never born. Although it had lived briefly, alongside her hopes, with her future across town in the house Leroy's wife had left.

We used protection. Leroy's feet were big and white by the swimming pool. His fingers probed the horizontal scar across his chin. Leroy never told her how he got it, and she liked that he didn't. Sandra envisioned Andrea taking her laps every morning in Leroy's in-ground, her long limbs slicing through the water, no sound, a predatory prepubescent blur of flesh and pink lycra. How could this have happened?

The condom must have broken. She wrapped her shawl over her shoulders, feeling the ice from his glass rattling in her stomach. He put the glass to his lips, two ice cubes with a last lick of gin, and sucked on them. He pressed his eyes shut, felt for the sunglasses on top of his slicked hair, pool wet. Leroy, it was an accident, but surely it's a good thing?

How?

Well, Andrea and I will be moving in soon. We'll be starting... our own family.

My wife is moving back in. He put the glass on the table, thud, and the wet around it grew like blood in a cloth. I'm sorry, Sandra. She just can't make it on her own.

What about me?

You've got Jack, Sandra. Old dependable.

What about—I can't just toss it away like a napkin. She dabbed at her eyes. Water everywhere. Blue eyes, blue pool, blue gin. Three miscarriages before Andrea. She hoped she would miscarry this one, too.

I'm not saying that. I'll pay for it, I'll take you. I want to be there for you through this.

And after this?

Sandra didn't blink too much, look too long, take things too far. At parties she sat in the corner and played the piano, hours and hours until her fingers numbed, until Leroy joked they should put out a tip jar, and she looked through him and asked him to make her a martini, yes, Jack makes a dreadful one, doesn't he? Four, Jack held up his four fingers and nodded at Leroy's wife, staggering like a doe across the room.

I'm sorry. Sandra pulled her hands from the keys, turned to Alice. My hands hurt. Her stomach still turned when she thought of leaving Leroy's that afternoon. She was dead then but something in her lived on and when she killed it, after a day in bed with towels pressed between her legs, her fingers still played, yearned for keys, for something. Jack bought roses, yellow, and that evening when Jack went back to his equations, she pushed the thorns against her stomach, her wrists, plucked the buds and ate them until she was sick. I'm sorry. I think I need to lie down.

Should I go? Alice stood up. The sheet music fanned outward and fell. The quarter notes, half notes, staffs lined the floor, Sandra's life exposed in a language unknown to Alice.

I don't know. Sandra remained at the piano, her brow wrinkled.

Do you want me to call your daughter? Alice straightened the music, made sure the pages were in order, refolded the cuff of Sandra's left shirtsleeve. Georgi. Sandra's breath was quick, a stab. It did not fill up her lungs, and she inhaled again. Alice drew her hand back, her face pink, as Sandra brushed the top of Alice's palm with her pinky.

Oh, dear, no, thank you. The first thing Andrea will do is move me down to Florida with her, in some awful assisted living or something. Sandra stood up. I was convinced that if I didn't do the blog she'd think I'd already gone half mad.

She worries about you.

She worries about herself. Andrea didn't want Sandra close by, where she'd have to drive her to the store, help her clean the windows. And why would she? Sandra had been too busy for Andrea.

Alice didn't look like Georgi. It was that she made Sandra feel like Georgi had.

I worry about my mother constantly, Alice said. Especially now that my father's dead.

I'm sorry, dear. Sandra touched Alice's shoulder. Her shoulder was warm through the fabric of her blouse. You're so young. I'm sure your father was, too.

Who is this? Alice held up the photo of Leroy. Your brother?

I brought this one out by accident. Sandra took the photo from her, cradled it in her palm and stood up.

Alice stood up with her. She put the envelope back in her bag, before Sandra could see what other photos she had. I hope you feel better. I really should go if you're unwell.

Mind you, it is not a physical sickness. Sandra went into the bedroom and put the photo in her nightstand. She felt Alice at the door, felt her eyes poring over Sandra's things. Her chaise lounge when she sometimes read or listened to the rain, the Hitchcock chair from the old house that did not go in the living room, the walnut armoire. Sandra sat on the bed. I should very much like to hear about your father, if you still have time.

I should go. Alice did not enter. I'll e-mail you a story to read, though—will it be too much trouble to read it on the laptop?

I suppose it shouldn't be. Sandra wrapped her arms around herself. She closed her eyes and felt her hands touching her shoulder blades. I should be open to new things. Won't Andrea be surprised at my sudden technological facility?

6.

She read Alice's stories in bed. It seemed luxurious, and intimate. She drank coffee and split a tangerine with her fingers, felt the coolness of the top sheet on her elbows. The story was about a veterinarian who had fallen out of love with her partner. At the end, the veterinarian begins to cry uncontrollably after euthanizing a particularly young, handsome Labrador retriever with inoperable brain cancer.

Is your ex a veterinarian? Sandra called Alice at seven o'clock on Monday morning because she felt she must know. Did your father die of brain cancer?

I'm assuming you've read my story?

Yes. The laptop was warm on her legs in the bed. She felt a tickle in her stomach at the sound of Alice's voice, close to her ear. The light was soft through the curtains, dreamy. She heard a coffee pot percolating and wondered what was in Alice's kitchen, whether she had a teapot. A spaghetti strainer. A wooden spoon. But this story comes from real experiences, yes?

Some of it. I guess most do.

Does your ex-lover date someone new? Sandra did not know why she was so demanding. Age had stripped her of patience, subtlety.

Not that I know of. She still calls now and then.

Why?

I don't know. Maybe there's still something there for us.

My lover went back to his wife. There was nothing left for us. She closed the lid of the laptop. I suppose you have studied other authors, and it sounds very professional, this one. Like a real story.

Did you like it?

I don't like most stories I read because they're about young people and I don't understand them. No one ever writes about older people.

I don't think that's true. If you come down to the bookstore where I work, you'll find plenty of memoirs and the like.

Memoirs talk about the past. No one cares about us now.

I don't think that's true.

It was true. She did not go out much anymore. The streets had changed and the stores had changed and the cars had changed and the clothes had changed and everyone was so young and they looked around her, through her. Unless they were being polite they did not see Sandra, they saw some old woman thrown on top of her and they mistook her for something small, frail, needing help. A stray.

The people from the grocery store delivered fresh fruits, vegetables, and she ate salads and soups, sometimes small cuts of meat. The driver came when she needed to go to the doctor. But mostly she played the piano and walked the block around her house, ever fearful of the new coffee shop, the Mexican restaurant that replaced the Jewish deli, the cell-phone store where the florist once was.

Listen, come to the bookstore later. I work from eleven to seven. I'll buy you a coffee and we'll find you some books to read, okay?

You make it sound like I'm a child. But perhaps she had been acting like one. All right. I'll come. For a little while. Your story... your story I enjoyed very much. I am sorry the veterinarian left you.

She isn't a veterinarian. She works at a library. But it doesn't matter.

You'll feel better, you know. She had not had a lover after Leroy. It was not because she loved Leroy more than anyone else. It had just been too much trouble. Not the secrecy, but the pain. She had driven the Jaguar out to the Tudor house, watched Leroy's wife herd their daughters outside to drive them to the swim club. It was cool for October, the girls' faces stretched and their eyes thin with petulance as they plopped in the back seat, clutching their duffels of swim things. Sandra followed them. It would be so easy to sit on the bleachers next to Leroy's wife, as the girls knifed through the chlorinated water, and mention that Leroy's dick curled to the left and didn't she find that most odd? Leroy's wife was suspicious of all of them, Jean and Georgi and Sandra, as was Sandra of Jean and Georgi. It had not surprised her later to find out that Leroy had had affairs with all of them, but by then it had been too much trouble to care. By then Andrea was into boys and there were dances to plan, dresses to buy and hem. By then Leroy's hair had begun to thin and Jack was his supervisor.

She did not go into the swim club that day. She went to the doctor's office, where she was headed in the first place. Jack could not get off work. There was the conference in Toledo and he needed to get his lecture done and make sure the young chemists were ready with their poster presentations. Couldn't she ask one of her friends? How about Jean or Georgi? But Jack, I need you. But Sandra, my dear, I just don't believe that it's possible for me to make it. And why not, then? Well, because I just don't believe the baby is mine.

But he brought home yellow roses. Why roses, why yellow. Why anything. Then he moved into the guest room. And Sandra stopped cleaning it.

Did it get better for you? Alice's voice was quiet.

It hurt less. Her voice was even quieter. Jack moved back into their bedroom when Andrea left for college. The war had been over for years. No one had won. They had simply stopped fighting.

7.

She decided on the light wool pants suit, slightly dated, gray suede gloves, grabbed her cane. Sometimes if she were out too long her hip would begin to ache slightly, her hamstring stiffen. Polio from when she was a child. She found the little nub of lipstick, Bois de Rose, that no one seemed to carry any longer, and drew her lips. The driver from the chauffer service came. It wasn't always the same driver but the drivers always acted the same way; respectful, fawning, ever mindful of their handsome reimbursement. Yes, how do you do, Ms. Holiday. Need anything else, ma'am? It's always good to see you. She waved off the hand extended to her, climbed in the back.

The bookstore was big. She had heard of the place from Andrea but had never gone. The large dome lights made people's skin look like wet powder, and the high ceilings and exposed ductwork reminded her of a factory. She scanned the aisles, filled with younger browsers, comfortable and absorbed by books or magazines. So much color packed in blond wood bookshelves.

She walked to the information desk. A girl in t-shirt and jeans, red hair chopped unevenly, looked up from the computer.

Is Alice here?

Alice Henry? I think she's stocking. Let me check for you. The girl pointed at the arc of counter where Sandra stood. Stay right here. As if she would wander off, incapable of figuring out where the best place to await such news would be. She watched the girl, her body too big for her clothes, walk a few aisles over and speak to someone hidden by the shelving. Sandra could see the words *some old lady* form on the girl's lips. She considered leaving, going home and canceling the blog project. When Alice Henry appeared at the information desk, open-faced and smiling like a moon-face doll, Sandra wanted to slap her.

You came. Alice grabbed some books behind the counter before taking Sandra's arm. I've got a fifteen-minute break.

Fifteen minutes? Sandra's grip on her cane tightened. I had the driver come and pick me up, drive all the way across town for fifteen minutes?

I'm sorry. I only have fifteen-minute breaks. I guess I should have made that clearer this morning. Coffee?

Yes, I guess you should have. Sandra sat down at the table. A plain coffee would be nice. Everything felt very big. She looked at the space around Alice's head, her arms, the way she walked to the coffee bar, the slight too-bigness of her jeans that was not oft-putting. She watched Alice in space, so light and compact and hard, and felt bad for subjecting her to the cramped dark of her condo. She wondered whether they should meet somewhere else from now on.

Alice returned with the coffees, her smile faint. She nudged one of the books toward her. So, I think you might like Alice Munro. And not because we share the same name.

Do you like working here? Sandra brought the long cylinder to her lips. It felt too big for her hand, the coffee scalding her beneath its thin cardboard skin.

It pays the bills, Alice shrugged. Sandra wondered if she hated working at the bookstore, thought it was beneath her. The universities didn't hire you to teach unless you had a book out. Alice had said as much during her last visit. She had a few stories published here and there, nothing like that, nothing yet, but she was working on it and Sandra supposed this was what people did while they were working on things.

Virginia Woolf. Alice pushed *Mrs. Dalloway* toward Sandra. I think you'll enjoy this very much.

What do you enjoy? Sandra moved the books back and forth on the table but did not open them. She was disappointed that Alice thought she was illiterate. But she was the one who picked the fight in the first place. She didn't know why she was so difficult, so angry. If she were younger she could blame it on her hormones, Jack. She dabbed her lips with her napkin. Alice coughed violently, her body pitching forward at the table. Dear, you have to get that checked. I have a good doctor.

I don't have health insurance.

I'll pay for it.

What? Alice put her coffee down with a thud. Sandra's jaw tightened. Had she said that? They both looked at the table. Sandra wanted to leave this happy, bland place as soon as possible. She hated Alice, hated that she was so young and careless.

Don't be silly. Alice was the first to speak. I quit smoking a little while ago. The coughing is just that. I'll go to the clinic if I have to.

Whatever you do, I want you to go, please.

Thanks. Alice touched Sandra's hand, still gloved, across the table. You're very kind. Sandra's hand went limp as Alice moved her fingers curiously over the digits, the spaces between them. A spoon fell to the floor, at another table, and their hands parted.

I guess your break is almost over. Sandra pressed on the cane and rose. I'll take these, then.

I still have a few minutes. Alice stood up. I'm sorry, I shouldn't have asked you to come. But I wanted to see you.

You shouldn't apologize. Sandra turned away, holding the books. Had she wanted to see her, or were they just words that one said?

Wait. I could take off. We're not busy.

Don't be silly. Sandra pulled her wallet from her purse. You can't afford to take off. And I've other appointments.

It's always good to see you. Alice walked Sandra to the counter.

Would you like to go to dinner? Sandra turned. She imagined going to Martick's together, a French meal. It seemed so urgent that her eyes grew teary. Tonight?

Tonight? Alice looked at the clock. I can't. I'm sorry. I have a date.

A date? Sandra found the counter with her hand, dropped the books on it. With who?

Lauren... my ex.

But I thought that...

Yes, Alice laughed, pulling her hair back in a ponytail. I did, too.

Do your coworkers think I'm your grandmother? Sandra asked. She would never come back here. There were so many places, she found, she never went back to.

What? Who said that? Sherrie? She had no business. Alice looked back toward the information desk.

She didn't. Sandra shook her head. It doesn't matter. She purchased the books that she had already owned, read, at some point in her life. She didn't want to disappoint Alice. And yet Sandra had gotten dressed, gotten the car, and not been given time for lunch, for dinner. Alice did not understand; perhaps Sandra had not explained how difficult it was for her to get out. Sometimes it was the pain in her ankles and elbows and hips and sometimes it was the pain of having nowhere to go. But here she had somewhere to go and it was over before she even had time to experience it.

The nursing home on Dowling Street. She motioned to the driver. She dropped the books on the seat and wiped her eyes and then picked up the books again. The nursing home smelled like shit. She supposed they all did. She took the elevator to the third floor, room 3C. He sat in his wheelchair by the corner. The first few times she visited last year she thought he remembered her because of the way his eyebrows arched, his lips parted. Why, you look great, gal. A sight for sore eyes.

She had spent a long time that first time, explaining how she had not forgiven him, merely felt sorry for him. She wouldn't wish so many strokes on her worst enemy. And he had nodded, that big head lolling about on his thin neck and hollow shoulders, a bowling ball on a toothpick, and she sat with him and played for him a little on the piano in the rec room, *Who can I turn to, when nobody needs me*, and he sure was a cad back then, sure, but you've always been a great gal, a great gal Sandy. He rubbed his finger against his chin and thanked her for coming.

She knocked on the doorframe to get his attention, cleared her throat, and he looked up at her.

Why, look at you, gal. What a surprise. He grabbed her hands. She felt the coldness of his fingers through her gloves. How long has it been? How do you like old Club Med here?

I brought you some books. She laid them on his nightstand. She opened the drawer and ran her hand along his linen handkerchiefs, shaving kit. She wondered if his daughters ever brought things, whether the nurses took them. She wondered what he would consider valuable, what he would remember as being valuable. For her, the brooch her mother had given her. She always wore it, tucked under the collar of her shirt, sometimes on a bra strap. Nothing he had ever given her. And yet here she was, and she didn't know why. Because he was alive, she supposed.

She shut the drawer as the nurse's aide ambled past her, overweight and sloppily tucked. She did not understand why no one took any time with anything anymore. Even with him. They had dressed him in a polo shirt and sweatpants. A small part of her mind was pleased that he was wearing sweatpants and diapers but the large part of her mind hated herself for it. She sat on the bed as the nurse brought his pills in a cup and wondered who might visit her at the nursing home, what mu-mu the overweight sloppily tucked nurse's aide would put on her body. I was just leaving.

Mr. Leroy, aren't you going to say goodbye to your wife? The nurse's aide pointed at her. They were all so stupid, the aides, and didn't last long.

I'm just a friend. She shook her head, picked the books up, and left without touching him. She put the books in the rec room and hurried out to the car, and before the driver could even open the door, his mouth, she told him to take her home.

When they arrived Sandra told him to come back in an hour. She made the reservation and opened her closet, looking for a dress. She pulled out the knit one, grey with a black belt that she last wore to someone's retirement dinner several years ago. She took some ibuprofen in the bathroom with a glass of milk and got in the shower and let the water fall over her until her skin felt puffy and warm and then she put lotion all over her skin, frowned at where it had loosened from her body like ripe fruit.

Martick's was crowded and dark, a big restaurant pushed into a small, windowless space of basement. The murmur of conversation, laughter, tickled her skin. The darkness stroked her.

I have a reservation. For one. She tightened her hands on her cane. The waiter showed her to a corner. She didn't mind being stowed away like some hat rack because she could see everyone from there. Younger couples, older couples, younger and older mixed together. She and Jack had come many times with their friends but that was a long time ago. She did not recognize the wait staff, the bartender, the artwork, the napkins. She knew what she wanted but she picked up the menu and made sure they still had it, the veal chop with girolles. She ordered a glass of Bordeaux.

She saw two women sitting together across the way. One touched the other's arm, laughed. She wondered if they were together, marveled that they could be so open about it. She certainly couldn't imagine a thing like that back in the day. Although it had happened.

There had been Georgi. Georgi in her strapless cocktail dress, her shoulders square and white like bricks of butter. Georgi always ran her hands through her hair as if she couldn't believe it was there, or so short, or so wavy, or so thick. She smoked cigarettes down to the filter and coughed when she laughed. You're quite a dame, Georgi, Leroy would joke and bum a Pall Mall on the patio. Isn't she, Sandra? Sandra would laugh. She had always suspected Georgi and Leroy but she did not know until later. She and Georgi didn't happen until later, after Leroy and Sandra, after Leroy and Georgi, but possibly before Leroy and Jean. Not that she cared at that point.

Sandra, I wish I was as talented as you. Georgi flicked her cigarette down as Leroy held the ashtray toward her. Click, click, click, she meandered, in heels, heavily across the patio to gather her drink. What about your tennis, Georgi? Leroy laughed, went to corral her, his collar open, tie, green and blue and gold stripes, unknotted. Sandra looked at his hand, open, the hairs on his fingers. If there was an Olympic event for double faults, Georgi would medal, wouldn't you, old girl? There's quite a dame, Georgi.

I hope he gets syphilis. Georgi lit another cigarette after Leroy went back to the party. I hope his dick falls off.

What's the matter, Georgi? Sandra didn't blink too much, look too long, take things too far. She patted Georgi's forearm. Come on, he's harmless.

I wish I were as nice as you, Georgi laughed. Drink spilled out of her glass and onto the patio. Somebody's gonna cut his dick off, and it may as well be me.

Why don't you lie down, Georgi? Sandra led her through the house to the guest room. Just sleep a few drinks off. Jack will drive you home if you need him to.

You have everything, Sandra—Jack, Andrea, the piano. Georgi's lips were full, pouty. You are quite a dame. Oh, God, Sandra, why are you crying? Did I say something wrong?

Of course not. Sandra shook her head, hand over her eyes. You flatter me and it's far from the truth.

Oh, Sandra. You deserve everything. Georgi's hand cupped Sandra's face. How about that? Sandra felt Georgi's body shift in the bed, her weight come up to her. Georgi kissed her. She smelled like smoke and vodka, heavy and wet in her mouth, and Sandra ran her hands through Georgi's hair and kissed her. So luxurious, thick, silky, Georgi's hair, like her shoulders, her waist. A silkiness she had not expected to feel, except on herself.

She had stupid thoughts, like she and Georgi would run away together on the train that night. They would go to Vermont and eat pancakes and maple syrup and take walks in the woods. Georgi closed her eyes and sank back into the guest bed. Sandra watched her sleep, watched their whole life together begin and end beneath Georgi's eyelids. She took Georgi's glass and threw it against the wall, where it prismed into a million pieces and when Jack questioned her the next day, she told him Georgi had dropped it.

The veal came and she picked up her fork. When one of the women from the table noticed her, Sandra raised her glass and nodded. The woman smiled, toasted back. Then Sandra slid the knife into the meat.

8.

Sometimes when Alice closed her eyes, she saw the woman in Sandra's pictures. She kept one picture in her bag, close to her. In it Sandra was sitting under an umbrella at the beach, a cottage behind her. *Southampton 1967.* Her legs were tucked under, firm and tan, her hair spilled over her shoulders, and her cheeks scrunched into a smile. Alice was in love with that woman. A book was open beside her, pushing onto the sand—Norman Mailer? Alice did not know why she thought Sandra had not already read Alice Munro and Virginia Woolf.

Alice wanted Sandra to know that she saw her, she wasn't invisible, that when she rounded the bookshelves and saw Sandra standing there in her suit at the information desk, waiting for her, that her stomach hurt and she was thrilled and scared that she knew such a woman. She wanted to love this woman, just as she loved the woman in the photo, but Sandra was so moody, so scarred with age, bitter with memory. Alice wanted to say all those things but she said nothing. After Sandra left the bookstore, she went into the bathroom and big, stupid tears formed in her eyes. It was not pity she felt. More that something had been lost, or taken, or was never hers to begin with, even though she realized with a ferocity that she had wanted it more than anything.

She was going out to dinner with Lauren. Because Lauren made more sense. Because Lauren had called and asked her to dinner. Because for the past 4 months Lauren had been in Alice's thoughts for thirty seconds out of each minute, it seemed. Because when Lauren had left Alice stayed with her mother for twenty-one days. She drank cocoa and ate Trix cereal for breakfast and lunch. She got in bed at midnight but did not fall asleep until three or four in the morning. She awoke at eleven and ate Trix for breakfast and lunch. She walked around the house and touched things, her mother's thimble collection, over a hundred in all. She preferred the one shaped like a castle. It was useless as a thimble but Alice liked to joke she had a fortress on her finger. Her mother's more expensive, older thimbles were plain. Invisible to Alice. She walked around the house and pulled out books from her father's collection of books on the Civil Warmemoirs and historical analyses and troop movements. She flipped through the pages, looking for forgotten bookmarks, paper scraps with her father's handwriting on them, some secret note to himself *reference with Battle of Fredericksburg in Lehman book p. 52* or *milk, prescriptions, birthday card.*

For twenty-one days Alice looked at her mother's and father's things and wondered how those things kept them together, the boxes of *National Geographic* magazines in the garage her mother had ordered her father to trash on many occasions but could now not part with herself, the coffee mugs her mother always seemed to bring home from work, and Alice wondered why her possessions and Lauren's, so neatly arranged and so complimentary, had not.

They went to the Afghani place though Alice could not afford it. She didn't want Lauren to think she suffered in any way without her monetary support, her love, although Lauren could easily enough figure Alice's bookstore salary equaled Ramen noodles, generic diet soda, a dingy walk-up on 21st.

I'm helping a woman ghostwrite her memoirs. Alice took a sip of wine. She had wanted to order by the glass but Lauren had insisted on the bottle. I upload everything to a blog with her pictures so her grandkids can learn about her life.

Does that interfere with your own writing? Lauren tore some bread from the loaf the waiter left.

Not really. I've got time for both. She pays really well. I find her more fascinating than I intended.

Well, you always attract fascinating people. Lauren held up her glass. To your magnetism.

Yes. Alice nodded. But she did not look at Lauren. She thought of Sandra's hands, cloaked in gloves, the triangle of her neck underneath the collar of her shirt, the base of her throat that she always tried to hide. To a point Alice had thought it ugly. Ugly as an abstract thing, a base of wrinkles. But it was Sandra's neck, Sandra so beautiful reading Norman Mailer in the Hamptons, who played the piano and calibrated Alice through wet blue eyes. And it could no longer be ugly to Alice. She thought of Sandra's traces of perfume, soap, mints. That she took the time to disguise herself from Alice with such things when Alice did not want her disguised.

Alice?

I'm sorry. Alice smiled apologetically. She did not force herself to think about Sandra. She just did. And slowly, over the days, it seemed that Lauren was not in her thoughts every thirty seconds on the minute but maybe once an hour, maybe twice. And Sandra? How many minutes, times?

I'm sorry. Alice shook her head again. I've been having the craziest thoughts lately.

Don't we all?

I don't mean to be rude. Alice looked into her glass. But it really fucking hurt when you left. We were together five years when you decided that you were in love with Hanne. But of course she didn't love you the way you thought, huh?

Alice, I...

And now you're crawling back. Isn't that why we're here, having dinner?

Is that what you think? Lauren blinked. Lauren had always acted like she was doing Alice a favor, that there were so many other women vying for her attention at the library, at yoga, at graduate school. I still care for you, Alice. I always have. I left Hanne, not the other way around. I missed you so much.

Alice had replayed this scene in her head many nights. Between tears, tea, and valium. Walking the apartment in the dark, pretending to hear Lauren rustling the sheets in the next room. But she had not expected to hear it.

I care for you, too, Lauren. But I'm not sure I can see you. I need to move on with my life. She'd called Lauren for days, weeks, after the breakup, begging her to come back. She would have given up so much. Now, she wondered what Sandra had eaten for dinner, whether she should wrap some of her Lamb Lawand and take it to her.

Lauren put down her wine glass. I miss you, Alice. I just got scared. Five years and we're so young and what if I go to grad school in Vancouver? You couldn't be that far from your mother. But I miss you. I thought we could just be patient and see where things went right now... or didn't.

I'm seeing someone else.

What? Who?

No one you'd know. Alice finished her drink, poured herself another. I just wanted you to know that.

They moved out of sync, glasses raised too jerkily, drank too quickly. Forks clinked against plates, hands reached for the same pepper bottle. They didn't order dessert. Alice walked toward the bus stop, and instead of taking the number 9 home, she took the number 13. It was late, she knew, but she knew she was going to see her.

9.

She got home from Martick's at eleven. She had not been out that late in a long time, had not seen the city dark, the streetlights. She wanted to see more. But not tonight. Her stomach was upset, unused now to heavy dinners.

The knock at the door frightened her. She waited for it to stop. It happened again. She had a bat that Elvin had left behind when he visited last. She found it in the closet and moved to the front door, noting the hollows and shadows of the living room, spaces where her body could lie, curled like a baby's fist.

Alice. Sandra pulled on the door and dropped the bat.

Oh, I'm sorry. Alice bent over and picked up the bat where it rolled between them. I shouldn't have been so thoughtless, coming here at night.

No, no, no—come in. I just got home.

I can see that. Alice looked at Sandra's dress, her eyes moving up and down. You look lovely.

I went out for dinner. She smiled slightly. Would you like something to drink?

No—don't go to any trouble. Alice stood in the doorway. I'm so sorry. I don't know what I was thinking, bothering you like this.

It's all right. Sandra went to the couch, patted it. Your mind is heavy?

No. Alice crossed the room, shaking off her coat and balling it up in her lap. No, it's rather light. Are you sure you don't want me to leave?

Yes, I'm sure. The nights were always the worst, when it was darkest and quietest. She couldn't play the piano because of the neighbors, and all she had were her memories. No matter what she did, she could not make them loud enough in her mind. To fill the dark. She hated that they were so soft, pastel chalks, interrupted by car horns, intestinal distress, her own inexplicable sadness.

Sandra, I feel so terribly about not going with you to dinner. Is that why you came?

Yes. Alice squirmed in the seat. It is. I had a terrible dinner with Lauren. I don't love her anymore. I wish I had gone with you.

Who don't you love anymore? Sandra asked. Her hands felt big and she did not know where to put them. The veterinarian?

Yes, Alice laughed. The veterinarian.

You're young, and pretty. You'll find someone else.

Thanks. Alice looked Sandra in the eyes. Coming from you, it means a lot to me.

Does it? Sandra spoke tonelessly. She leaned forward, pretended to wipe some dust off the end table. She could hear her heart in her throat and wondered whether Alice could, too. I would play you something, but it's late.

I don't need you to entertain me. Alice hugged her coat. But maybe we can talk. It's funny that I'm helping you with your memoirs when I feel like I don't even know you. I mean, I know... the chronology of your life. But I don't know what you think.

No one ever wants to know what one really thinks. Sandra shook her head. You have your expectations of me, and if you're wrong you'll become disillusioned.

Do you actually believe that?

Yes. I've been around the block a few times, as they say.

Well, what do you think I think about you?

I don't know. Sandra touched her head. Her hair was thin. She always found it clumped in the drain when she showered. You think I'm judgmental and rigid. You think I live in the past.

What do you think of me?

Sandra sighed. I thought you were insincere, nice to me, like everyone else, because I paid you. Because it's not a good investment to put time into someone who needs and needs from you and is just going to die. But now I'm not sure. I don't know what you want from me.

Everyone dies. Alice shrugged. Didn't you once say that?

Yes. We've both watched people die. Me more than you, of course. My husband. Some of my friends have died, or they're slowly rotting away. And I'm just waiting my turn.

Well, I guess we agree on that.

On what?

That you lived once. And that you don't anymore.

When Georgi died it had been such a shock. She was the first one. They had stopped talking so many years before, after Georgi had married for the third time. Before that, whenever Georgi drove Sandra to the club she could hear the gin bottle rattling around in the glovebox of Georgi's Pontiac. Henry is a prince, Sandra. Did I tell you he is taking me to Bali for Christmas? You have to go to Bali, Sandra. Just don't use your left hand for anything when you're there—the left hand to them is sacred. Georgi took the curve too fast, and Sandra curled her hand over her door handle, gripped. What's the matter with Jack, anyway, Sandra? I know he can afford to take you places.

It's easy for you to say—you're still young. Sandra sighed, found a balled-up tissue in her robe. Alice took off her glasses. Sandra wondered whether she had been crying. When I get up in the morning, I never know if everything is going to work. And I started to find these damn tissues everywhere. I'm becoming my mother.

Georgi said her knee was acting up but Sandra knew she was just too drunk to play. They sat in the café, their tennis rackets leaning against their chairs, watching younger women in whites move like gazelles across the warm-baked green asphalt. The white lines were striking white, painted each year, even as the asphalt cracked. Like a made-up old floozy, Georgi laughed. Sandra ordered an iced tea and a chicken salad sandwich. Georgi had a highball and a club turkey. Did you hear, Sandra, she finally left Leroy, that son of a bitch. Caught him with Jean. I just don't understand how Jean fell for it, his shtick.

Why not? Sandra dipped her spoon halfway into her soup. Cream of broccoli. It looked like baby vomit. We did.

What was your mother like? Alice leaned her head against the couch, the caramel of her hair splayed across a cushion.

My mother was a very strong-hearted, unsentimental woman. She was very strict with me and my sister Clarice, but I was thankful for it. She hugged me at my wedding, and when I had Andrea. That was it. I was never very affectionate with Andrea, either. She resented me terribly for it.

Why weren't you affectionate with her?

If you come to expect a certain amount of affection, you begin to crave it. You make unwise decisions for it.

My mother hugged me all the time.

Is that why you're hugging your jacket now? Sandra smiled, stood. Here—let me hang it up.

Outside the club Georgi dropped her keys by the Pontiac.

I'll drive. Sandra pressed against Georgi. She grabbed Georgi's hand overtop the door handle. Please. She slid in the driver's seat past Georgi and fiddled with Georgi's keys.

Oh Sandra, you're never any fun. Georgi got in on the passenger side, pulled on the radio knob. *Do you know the way to San Jose, I've been away so long.* Come to Bali without Jack. We can do girl stuff.

Alice met Sandra by the closet. She moved so quickly, from couch to closet, that Sandra dropped the coat.

I've got it. Alice threw it onto the couch and then put her arms around Sandra.

Sandra leaned over and cupped Georgi's right cheek in her left hand, brushed her left cheek with her lips. She could smell Georgi's hair, her breath.

Sandra, stop. Georgi pushed at her.

Sandra stood stiffly, feeling Alice against her.

Shh. Sandra held onto Georgi. *I may go wrong and lose my way.* Sandra, stop. Georgi pushed hard and Sandra threw the car into gear, her hands trembling, heart beating. *And there you are without a friend.* She would throw up if she stopped. She put her hand on the wheel and gave it gas. *You pack your car and ride away.*

Georgi smoked a cigarette, hummed, searched for something in her purse. Sandra thought of old shoes, dirty napkins, white chipped coffee mugs at the diner where she sometimes did the crosswords, and the tears worked their way back into her head.

Remember to get back to me about Bali. Georgi leaned out of the driver's window after Sandra got out and Georgi switched places.

Are you sure you don't want to come in and lie down, Georgi? Sandra put her hand over her heart. I worry about you drinking and driving.

Are you saying you think I'm an alcoholic? Georgi threw her cigarette out on the street.

No, I'm not saying that—

At least I'm no dyke. Georgi stared straight ahead, waiting, waiting for Sandra to say something.

Sandra turned and walked toward the door. She listened for the car to pull away, the crunching of the asphalt under the tires. She heard it idling, kept walking. She got to the front door, the colonial red that was special ordered, the brass doorknocker, and she put her hand on the cold knob. Ten seconds, twenty. She turned, and Georgi drove away.

Sandra could smell Alice's hair, caramel splayed, feel the rising and falling of her breath. Ten seconds, twenty. She touched Alice's head, her back.

Why are you crying? Alice held her by her arms. Sandra shook her head. She had played the piano all afternoon after Georgi left, Barber and Schumann, and forgotten to pick Andrea up from school. The call from her teacher, Andrea crying in the front yard as Jack stormed up the sidewalk to the house. She'd never seen him so mad. He held her by her arms and shook her. What, you making a little bird's nest with Leroy, now his wife's flown the coup? Is he more important than your child now? She shook her head. No, Jack, of course not. Answer me. He shook her.

Jack left a mark. Georgi had explained it to her once, how her second husband Redmond knew how to slap her and not leave a mark. Sandra sat in the kitchen and held a towel to her face. Mommy slipped in the kitchen, honey. Don't cry. She pushed Andrea, tear-streaked, out the door with Jack for ice cream.

I'm not crying, she answered, shaking her head. It's getting late.

Come. Alice held her by the arms, guided her across the living room toward the bedroom. Sandra lay back on the bed perfectly still, slipping off her shoes, watching Alice walk over to the other side and lie down beside her. Sandra looked at the ceiling, her breath shallow.

Should I leave? Alice asked.

You can stay, if you'd like. Sandra spoke to Alice's voice, her eyes on the ceiling. It's late.

Am I making you uncomfortable?

I won't be able to sleep with you here.

Well, I should go. Alice sat up in the bed.

No. Sandra grabbed Alice's wrist. That's not what I meant.

It was easier back then, with Leroy. Sandra was attractive, firm, aroused. Sandra thought about Alice seeing her body, the sags and stray hairs and age spots she saw every morning, in the shower. If Alice was even interested. And why on earth would she? Alice turned on her side, but Sandra didn't let go of her wrist.

It was easier back then, with Leroy. It was what one did. Men and women needed no justification. No barriers, not even marriage, constrained them. It was what one did, men and women. If you were women together or men together there had to be so many other reasons—no men, no women, childhood trauma, alcoholism. Insanity. And for women of different ages, there was no justification. But she did not let go of Alice's wrist.

10.

Alice felt Sandra's fingers, tight and then loose and then tight again, drifting, awake. She had wanted to kiss her but didn't know how Sandra felt. What she herself would even feel about it, tomorrow. But she wanted to kiss her now. In the soft gray-pink of the bedroom Alice leaned over, touched the skin on Sandra's cheek with her lips. It was cold, ridged with light valleys and dunes. Sandra stirred, her nose wrinkled, and Alice retreated to her side of the bed.

Later, the morning painted light through the blinds onto the ceiling. Alice turned to look at Sandra, still sleeping. She could see Sandra's entire life under her eyes. Photos were scattered on the chaise lounge next to the bed. Alice slipped the circle of Sandra's hand and gathered them. They were of Sandra and another woman with short dark hair, a face bare and smooth as a field, round white teeth, thin-lipped smile. But the woman had gravity to her, a weight that made Sandra feel gauzy. In each photo the dark-haired woman held a drink like an anchor. Sandra's neck was thin and long and tucked itself shyly into her collarbones, peeking out of the tailored white shirt. She smiled, hinting at great secrets or amusement but distance, reticence.

I didn't get a chance to put those away yesterday.

I'm sorry. Alice put the pictures back into the envelope as Sandra sat up in bed. I had no right.

Are you hungry? Sandra eyed her, her eyes blue water brightness. Alice felt wet inside, her heart slippery.

Alice knew a place a few blocks over. Sandra insisted she could walk, prodding her cane at the sidewalk, as if the streets would suddenly collapse and swallow her. She wore dated Chanel sunglasses. At the street corner she applied chapstick. A blur of cars whiffed the air before them. Alice hooked her arm into Sandra's and stepped from the curb.

I'm not going to fall. Sandra untangled from Alice. Alice wondered whether she had been projecting something onto Sandra. A mutual interest. She wanted to go home and crawl into her own bed. There, she knew where the sheets bunched up, which side squeaked when one sat up.

I'm sorry, Sandra. I didn't mean to imply you needed my help.

And will you please stop apologizing? Sandra pulled at the red scarf that covered her hair. Alice thought she might cry. She would blame it on the wind. At the restaurant the smell of maple syrup seeped its way into Alice's stomach. She concentrated on the white tablecloths and the chatter of silverware and glasses as the server helped Sandra into a chair. Sandra undid her scarf and shook her head lightly, running her hand through her hair. She scanned the menu, back and forth, back and forth, and Alice thought about Sandra's bed. Had they made the bed? She could not remember. She felt heat on her cheeks and brought the glass of water to her lips.

Have you thought about what you'd like? Sandra glanced up at her. What do you recommend?

The waffles are good. The omelets too, but you might have to wait a while.

I don't have anywhere to be. Sandra put her menu on the table.

Alice ordered the waffles with nuts and a side of yogurt and coffee and Sandra ordered a vegetable omelet with tea. The water bled brown as Sandra dabbed her teabag and Alice brought her coffee, too hot, to her lips. She fought down the searing sip, her eyes shut, and when she opened them a woman holding a can of Sunkist soda walked past the restaurant and she thought of drinking Sunkist soda in Virginia Beach with Heather. When they were ten, Heather and Alice would kiss and pretend they were married. Sometimes Heather would be the husband and sometimes Alice. But when they were fourteen, they didn't kiss anymore. Although Alice still wanted to.

Come out in the water. Heather's body bounced tight, brown, smelling of Hawaiian Tropic, in front of her. Alice had often thought at night about the perfect circle of Heather's breasts, about cupping them in her hands and feeling the puckered nipple between her fingers. What are you waiting for?

Alice was not a good swimmer. At the Y she had sunk to the bottom of the pool like a brick, a brick with arms flailing.

Come on. Heather grabbed her wrist. Their feet flirted with hot sand, recoiled from the cold surf.

More water? The waiter tipped the pitcher to her empty glass. Alice nodded.

Are you all right, dear? You're positively parched. Sandra bent her head, held her tea. Did you drink too much wine last night?

No. The water was so cold, but she didn't want Heather to let go of her. She saw the boys, Trevor and John, ahead of them, bouncing over the waves, and she wanted them to get carried off far to sea, their big heads like beach balls floating into the horizon. But Heather let go; her body disappeared into a wave, and Alice searched for the bottom with her feet.

Did you sleep?

I think so.

Her arms, legs searched through the layers of water for something to anchor onto as the current pulled her further out to sea. Now she was beyond the boys. And they stared at her dumbly as Heather cried at her, her mouth a perfect O. Sometimes she still woke up at night with Heather's expression burning in her mind. As if she had been the one who died. She struggled to get back, the beach, the boys, Heather disappearing as she took in water, the waterline filling above her eyes.

You're so quiet.

The arm found her waist and pulled her back. One of the boys. Trevor. He hovered over her on the beach, the saltwater dripping from the silver crucifix on his neck, droplets hiding in the wisps of hair at the base of neck.

Is it me? Sandra brought her teacup to her lips.

You're so lucky. Heather pouted at the pizza parlor while Trevor and John stood in line for pizza. I wish Trevor would save me.

No. Alice shook her head. But it was Sandra. It was everything. Everything was so wrong. People at the restaurant did not look at them, or they looked with patronizing smiles. Like when Alice took her mother out to dinner. Tell me about the woman in the picture.

I thought. Sandra choked suddenly, her eyes full of so much water. She put her napkin to her face. I thought that I loved her once.

The food came—waffles fluffy and crispy with nuts curled and bursting on top. Alice filled the little squares with maple syrup, felt reluctant to break down the walls between them, so pretty and self-contained. She looked at Sandra's half-moon of egg.

Looks too lovely to eat, doesn't it? Sandra's knife hovered above the yellow-white skin, flanked by golden fried boxes of potato. She slid the steel in surgically, opening the wound by tilting her hand this way, that.

But you didn't? The coffee was cooler, or maybe she had just gotten used to its heat.

Didn't what?

Didn't love her?

I suppose time lends perspective to these things. She carved egg into a perfect triangle, held it up to her face. I supposed I wanted to be loved. And maybe I did love her. But it was a foolish thing.

Why? Did she not love you?

I don't think it matters, whether she loved me or I loved her. It's not like we were going to run away together. You just can't fight the realities of the time.

What about now? Alice plunged her knife into the rows of perfect maple squares. Could you be with her now?

She's dead.

The syrup leaked onto the plate, slow and translucent brown. Alice tried to collect it onto her fork, but some of it would be lost. She wanted to pick up the plate and lick the syrup. Instead she touched it with her pinky, brought it up to her lips while she handled her coffee mug.

Was she the last?

The last woman?

The last person you loved? Alice wiped the plate with a wedge of waffle. The syrup disappeared, unsatisfying, into the sponge triangle.

I don't want to talk about it anymore. She pushed her plate to the side, squeezed her napkin with both hands.

Alice asked the waiter for two boxes. She wondered if she would eat the waffles, later, whether she would want something else.

I'll pay. Sandra placed an American Express on the table. Thank you for taking me out.

Alice nodded. She felt hungry, cheated. She wondered whether Lauren had called, changed her mind. She peeked into her open purse on the floor, at her phone.

On the way back Sandra tapped her cane on the crosswalk. Alice didn't take Sandra's arm at the intersection, played with her iPhone instead.

I have tickets, Sandra blurted. They stood in the lobby of Sandra's place. I have tickets to the symphony. I'm a subscriber. I mean, I don't go much, but I like to support them so I buy a subscription and sometimes I donate the tickets. I would love it so much if you'd go with me. There's one next week—Beethoven's Piano Sonata No. 8 and Tchaikovsky's Symphony No. 6.

Okay. Alice smiled, and whatever had sat between them at brunch had wandered off down the lobby.

I'm delighted. Sandra clasped her hands on top of her cane, eager. And sorry.

Why are you apologizing?

I feel awkward... and I've been rude... I don't know why. Perhaps I just... imagine things. She let go of the cane. It fell back against her leg as she cupped Alice's shoulders, patted her back, their faces close. I'll call you about the symphony. I'm sorry. I have to go.

Before Alice could say anything Sandra retrieved her cane and walked toward the elevator. Alice left so that when Sandra turned in the elevator she would not have to see her again.

11.

Sandra had wanted to be alone hours ago. To digest what had happened the night before. If anything had happened. Why the quick of her blood moved through her fingers, in her ears. The memory was vague. Perhaps a dream, of Alice's lips against her cheek. Was it a kiss Alice would give to her mother? In her bedroom she sat on the sheets, crumbled, faint with sleep. She put her hand where Alice's body had been, tried to remember the shape and heft of it. Unlike Jack's. It had been ten years since anyone had slept on the left side of the bed. She wondered whether she had begun to snore, had developed any odd body tics. Whether she smelled. Was her nightgown too outdated? Alice had slept in her clothes, shoes off, above the covers, as did Sandra.

She picked up the phone, dialed Andrea.

Do you think I'm too old to date?

Mother, why are you asking? Have you met a nice man?

I suppose I speak more hypothetically. I know that it would

have been difficult initially, but your father has been dead for ten years now.

You never loved Daddy, anyway.

That's not true. All parents argue. We were fond of each other at the end.

So why now?

I don't know. Why not?

Maybe I'll get to read about him on the blog, your mystery man?

I don't think so. Sandra tried to remember whether she and Jack kissed in front of Andrea. Certainly during Christmas, Sandra's birthday. Jack always smelled like menthol cough drops. She could not eat them to this day. Be quiet, or I'll vaporize you. He would open his mouth wide and breathe on her. She'd find cough drop wrappers in the ashtray by the bed, on the kitchen table, stuck between the bench seat cushions of the Cadillac. For years after his death she found them still, in the garage, in the trunk of the car, in a box filled with old issues of *The Journal of Biological Chemistry*. At first they were an annoyance, but as she began to find them less she hoped to find them more. Once at night, a few weeks before she sold the house, she went into the basement and probed through cobwebbed corners, the lint screen of the dryer, underneath the water heater. She sat on the tiled floor, which was cold and cracked and smelled faintly of mold, gasoline, and it was the last time she remembered crying. Sometimes at the store she fingered them, brought the package to her nose. But she could not buy them, sucked on the Swiss cough drops when she felt ill.

When are you coming to see me?

I'm not sure—the kids have been sick. Dan is working so much.

So probably not until a long time.

Well, you could always come and see us. It would be easier, since there is one of you and so many of us.

So typical of Andrea. Making her take an entire travel day to Florida. Carting luggage, walking through airports, ripe for mugging. Andrea had come up, stayed exactly three days for Jack's funeral, the children bumbling through the house, shrieking. Why couldn't Andrea's mother-in-law watch them? Andrea arranged to have Jack's work desk shipped to Florida. She sat on the patio, talking to Dan, the father of Beatrice and Elvin, on her cell phone, leaning on the wall where Georgi leaned, sitting on the patio furniture where Leroy sat.

Why did Sandra live in the past? Perhaps she still lived where she stopped living.

Do you think I'm too old?

To fly? Mother, they'll put you in the front. You'll be fine.

No, I mean, to date.

I don't know. I guess it's up to you. Do you want to date?

I don't know. I miss… people.

After Jack died, after Andrea took the desk and some of her old toys back to Florida, Sandra would call the driver and she sat in the back while he drove, past the old grocery store where the bag boys hugged the paper sacks against their chests and followed you to your car, to the music shop where she bought sheet music, the post office, where she sometimes mailed Jack's papers if he did not have an editorial assistant that semester. The corner store, now Indian takeout, where Sandra bought Jack cigarettes sometimes, Vantage, where she used to buy condoms. The Hutzlers where she bought some of Andrea's dresses, some of her own. She sat in the back and she told the driver to go to those streets that she knew and sometimes he would take shortcuts and they would pass new places but Sandra didn't look.

*   *   *

She gave the driver the directions to Alice's apartment, and he went north into the city. She looked at the Starbucks coffee houses and Panera eateries and corner liquor stores and people on street corners, people with dogs, going places, and she was going to Alice's, and she felt good. Her wine-colored cocktail dress still fit, and she was able to cover her shoulders with a silk wrap. She checked in her clutch for the tickets.

Alice's building was a brownstone, a three-floor walkup of six apartments. She wondered if she would have to get out and ring the bell, but then Alice appeared at the door. She wore a black dress underneath a belted trench coat. Her hair was up, away from the white moon of her face.

Good evening, Miss Golightly. Sandra scooted over on the seat.

Oh. Alice smiled, her dimples big. I left my tiara on the sink, Mr. Varjak. She shut the door and Sandra adjusted her wrap. Am I dressed all right for the symphony?

You look beautiful. Sandra patted Alice's shoulder, her stomach funny. Much nicer than most of the students who come. At least I didn't have to tell you not to wear jeans.

They took their seats in the box and Alice read her program, although Sandra could tell her everything she wanted to know if she just asked. Sandra looked at Alice's naked arm holding the page. Her own arm had been like that until she was sixty-five, smooth, pale, nearly hairless. Then she woke up one morning, looked in the mirror to wash her face, and she was old. Her face was cracked and pale, mottled pink white. The skin had loosened from her chin, her neck. Her hands hurt, her shoulder. The suddenness of it all shocked her. She stopped looking in mirrors, at her reflection in glass. But then people began to look through her, around her, and she wondered whether she had cursed herself into being invisible. She began to drum her hand on store counters, tap her cane, clear her throat. Andrea called her impatient, rude. Then, at some point, she just stopped making noise. Going out. She breathed shallow under her own covers.

Is the Beethoven hard to play? Alice asked.

It's a little difficult, but one can learn it. Mozart is easier, I think.

Will you play it for me later?

Tonight? Sandra gripped her program.

No... I didn't mean literally tonight. The lights dimmed, the musicians stopped tuning, and Sandra was thankful Alice could not see her hands shaking.

Beethoven was a young man, twenty-eight when he wrote *Pathétique*. He was already going deaf. When Sandra was twenty-eight, she wore her hair long. Andrea was five, in preschool. The house was quiet. For their eighth anniversary Jack had bought her a new stove, Andrea a Suzy Homemaker. In the afternoons after school Andrea would stir the air in the baking tin and then put the tin in the green oven with the pink range and a minute later she would take out the tin and serve the air on the little plastic plate. Devil's food, Mommy. Andrea's grin was perfect, a row of little corn teeth. For you. Sandra bit into the air and licked her lips, nodded her head.

She had wanted a new piano. Of course, the mahogany upright was serviceable. They had bought it cheaply, right after their wedding, from a widow who lived in their apartment building. But she had seen the Steinway at Schoemann's when she bought some sheet music a few months before. The owner let her play a little sonata, and another customer asked her to play some Rodgers and Hammerstein. If she could have this piano in the house, her lover, while Andrea was at school, she would ask for nothing more. She would never raise her voice to Jack. She would have sex three times a week. She would pretend to be blissfully happy. And maybe she would be.

But maybe she was greedy; she did get the Steinway eventually, for their twenty-fifth anniversary. But she had not needed the oven. The Maytag they already owned was serviceable, had come with the house. But Jack had seen the oven at the appliance store downtown, gleaming in the window. The salesman told him his wife could cook a rack of lamb in fifteen minutes. Jack did not know that Sandra could already cook a rack of lamb in the Maytag in fifteen minutes but that she had chosen not to. With the right equipment, perhaps he thought, she would be blissfully happy. Or pretend to be.

The pianist moved into the adagio cantabile. She straightened up, determined not to miss any more. The second movement was slower than the first. The chords, deliberate, pressed into her ears. Sandra fingered the Tahitian pearls around her neck. She didn't know why she wore them instead of her saltwater pearls. At several thousand dollars, they were much too expensive, too special, to wear them to just anywhere. Yet when she was dressing they were the first thing she picked up. They were not a gift from Jack; she bought them as an indulgence in Hawaii, an indulgence he didn't particularly care for, maybe because he had bought her the much cheaper saltwater pearls the winter before. They meant so many things to her, things that were reflected in the eyes of others here who knew the price and power of them. She understood this music, this symbolism, where everything means something, superiorly or inferiorly, in relation to everything else.

She did not understand her attraction to Alice. Alice probably wouldn't know the difference between Tahitian pearls and freshwater ones and probably preferred the oyster shells they came in above everything else. And here Sandra was, wearing her best pearls. To impress her?

She pivoted. Alice's eyes were closed. She brushed Alice's elbow softly, feigning accident. Alice opened her eyes and looked at her, moving her arm off the chair rest so that Sandra could have it. Sandra looked away, embarrassed. She glanced at Alice again, realized she had been watching her. Alice turned slowly back to the orchestra, unashamed of being caught. Sandra coughed, covered her mouth. The tickle in her throat spasmed her body, and she leaned forward. She felt Alice's hand lightly on her arm and froze. When she finally moved her eyes toward Alice, she saw the thing, white and waxy in Alice's palm. A cough drop.

12.

Sandra did not take the cough drop. She closed Alice's palm over it and pushed it back toward her. Alice had taken so much care tonight, with her dress, her makeup, her nails. But Sandra seemed offended by the cough drop, and Alice wondered whether she should have come. Her stomach felt funny and her cheeks were hot and she wondered whether she blew it with Lauren. She could not hear the music because Sandra, although not touching her, was all over her, her presence drowning out her thoughts and the music and she was so stupid for feeling the way she did about Sandra. She needed to teach her how to administer the blog so she could end it. She could find another part-time job or maybe Lauren would try again and they could move back in together and she could forget everything that happened between the break of them.

During intermission she excused herself and went outside and smoked the emergency cigarette she had in her purse. She could see Sandra through the glass doors of the lobby waiting for her, sitting straight on a bench, her eyes ahead, lips tight.

She wanted to walk behind Sandra and put her arms around her. She wanted to be that woman in the pictures, the woman whom Sandra loved, maybe. She wanted to be the woman Sandra loved, surely.

Are you enjoying the concert? Sandra asked when Alice returned. She did not make mention of Alice's smoking.

Yes. Alice held out her hand to help Sandra up. Surprisingly, Sandra took it, eased herself from the bench. You're the best date I've had in a long time.

Sandra blinked, once, twice, but did not relinquish Alice's hand. They went back to the box and sat down. Alice let go of Sandra's hand but when the lights dimmed and the musicians stopped tuning Sandra took it again and Alice did not hear anything but she wanted to so that if she ever heard this music again, on the radio, in a movie, she would get butterflies in her stomach and think of Sandra beside her, holding her hand.

After the concert the car was waiting. When Sandra gave the driver her own address Alice did not correct her. She watched the neighborhoods change into slightly more upscale groceries, boutiques, Sandra's condo. She followed Sandra through the lobby, which smelled like flowers from an aerosol can, to the elevator and watched her push the button for 12. She tried to think of something interesting to say about the concert that didn't make her look stupid and that didn't reveal that she had not heard most of it.

My husband, Jack, ate cough drops all the time, Sandra said, between the dings for floors nine and ten. Even when he didn't need to. Now, I don't eat them at all.

It's okay, Alice answered, and the doors opened. She followed Sandra inside. Sandra walked into her bedroom and sat at the edge of her bed, letting her program, her purse drop on the night table.

I can go. Alice pulled the belt on her coat.

If I wanted that, I would have told the driver to take you home. Sandra folded her hands in her lap. Alice let her arms, straight, fall from her coat. She folded it carefully and put it in the chair by the bed. Then she sat beside Sandra.

I miss Jack sometimes, Sandra said when Alice took her hand. I shouldn't say that. Not right now. I shouldn't say anything.

Alice wondered if they didn't say anything maybe what would happen would not be real, and it would be easier for them. She stood up and turned off the lights, felt for the bed in the darkness. She wondered if she should think about Sandra in the Hamptons or think about her now or think about Lauren. Perhaps she should not think at all. She felt Sandra's hand on her face, her fingers on her cheek and her chin and lips. She put her hands on Sandra's shoulders, soft, round. She pushed them, gently, and Sandra lay back on the bed. Alice tested her weight in Sandra's arms, pushed up on her knees so she would not smother her. Sandra collected Alice's hair in her hands and swept it behind her head and there was nothing between them except eyes, lips, noses. Alice leaned in and kissed her.

When Sandra's lips opened her breath was warm, wet. Alice touched the triangle at the base of Sandra's neck and felt the cartilage underneath. She kissed Sandra's lips and her face and her neck and her shoulder and the inside of her elbows. She thought about how, when she was Sandra's age, not even Sandra's age, Sandra would be dead.

Alice pulled away, lying on her side. Sandra took her hand.

Will you stay the night?

Alice wondered, if it came down to it, if she would always have to stay the night at Sandra's because her building did not have an elevator.

Yes, Alice answered. She went to the bathroom and took off her dress, her stockings, arranging them on a hanger Sandra had told her would be on the shower rod. She opened Sandra's medicine cabinet, noted the Oil of Olay, the prescriptions for osteoporosis, cholesterol. Tylenol. Ex-Lax. Eye drops.

When Alice returned Sandra had changed into a nightgown, long and sleeved. She moved to Alice and Alice's hands rose to her chest but Sandra took them, peeling them away and looking at her.

Why? Sandra asked, when Alice struggled against her. You're beautiful.

Alice shook her head. She did not know whether she was supposed to feel sexy or modest. Whether they were supposed to have sex or lie in each other's arms. She sat on the bed and took off her bra and pulled the blankets over her.

Are you waiting for me to go first? Sandra laughed, standing by the bed, the space around her eyes and mouth wrinkling. Well, I guess it's always good to check the expiration date.

Sandra pulled her nightgown over her head. There were hollows in her body where memories had been, names and places and dates but they had eroded, dwindled down to the bone and only the memory of them remained. An incongruity of bone and skin met at joints, ribs, like a folded chair that could no longer fold because it was broken. Alice did not want to look. She supposed over time she would get used to looking. But right now she did not want to look.

You're not a piece of meat, Alice smiled and turned away.

You need to see what you're getting into. Alice heard Sandra pick up her nightgown and slide into bed. Or not getting into.

Alice knew it didn't have to be anything more than just tonight, just kissing, but it was. It was about Sandra giving something to Alice for the promise of a future. When Alice and

Lauren lived together they talked of the future vaguely, assuming it was as far away as their death.

You are worried because I am so much older, Sandra said, and Alice turned to face her. Has it occurred to you that I am worried because you are so much younger?

I'm sure we're both worried. Alice put her hands above the bedspread. But we're here.

13.

The car came with Sandra. Alice was nervous. She had read many times before, at places, but she had not read with Sandra listening. She went to the bathroom and searched for some aspirin in her cabinets to stem the headache but could not find any. The headache was bulging out of her temple and she pressed her finger to it.

The knock startled her. She hurried across the living room and looked through the door's keyhole.

Sandra. Alice flung the door open.

I wanted to see your apartment. She leaned heavily on the cane, breath heavy through her nostrils. Before your reading. Is that all right?

There's not much to see. Alice watched Sandra move past her into the living room. There was a yoga mat still on the floor in front of the television, a bowl from which she had eaten canned soup for lunch on the table. Books overstuffed particleboard bookshelves. Dust covered everything. I'm sorry you had to come all the way up here.

Why? Sandra turned from where she stood in the middle of the living room. She was wearing a red belted dress with a low scoop neck. Instead of a scarf she wore a garnet necklace. Alice walked toward her and kissed the triangle of her neck.

I didn't mean that. Alice's hands found Sandra's small waist. It's just that...

I'm too frail, too old to visit you? Sandra moved from Alice's embrace to the bedroom. Is that what you meant?

No. Alice pressed her hand to her head. She told some friends she was bringing a new friend to the reading. A new friend? they repeated, smiled. So coy? We should go. It's getting late.

Sandra stepped back into the living room and smiled. Her hair was soft, white, styled with a hairdryer, lips drawn dark. Alice thought of her in her bathroom on the other side of town, putting on her earrings, brushing her teeth. Sandra moved toward Alice and touched her on the cheek. I should behave; this is your night.

On the stairs Alice walked down backwards, in front of Sandra. Sandra pressed her cane on each step, her hand on the railing. They would be late. Alice was upset that Sandra had not thought of this. That she would live beyond her capabilities for Alice and that it would upset things.

The reading was in a little bookstore, not the one that Alice worked. One that sold poetry chapbooks and independent-press titles. The kind of place Alice would have preferred to work, if she could afford to. She held out her hand for Sandra to get out of the car, dropped it when she was upright. She felt her cheeks get hot and patted Sandra's shoulder. Sandra kept her hand at her side. It had been different with Lauren, with the other girls. Perhaps because it had not been such a big deal. There were boys with boys and girls with girls in college, high school, even. But there had never been this.

Lauren had always come to Alice's readings, but she had not expected her tonight. And yet there she was, sitting in the front row, in a denim skirt and a wine-colored velour jacket. The one Alice had always liked. They had not talked since dinner, since they awkwardly said their goodbyes and parted. Maybe Lauren was just curious, whether Alice really was seeing someone.

Lauren stood when she and Sandra approached the first row. Alice. How are you? Lauren looked at Sandra, for a second, maybe two. She held her palm to her open chair. I'm sorry— would you like my seat, ma'am?

Thank you. Sandra lowered herself down, slide her cane underneath.

This is Lauren, Alice said to Sandra.

Oh, the veterinarian? Sandra smiled, looking up.

Yes. No. Alice smiled back, turned to Lauren. She works at a library. Sandra studied Lauren, her watery blue eyes raining all over her, measured drops. Lauren nodded and smiled at Sandra before looking back to Alice. Lauren, this is Sandra. Sandra Holiday.

A pleasure. Lauren held out her hand and smiled at Sandra's shoulder, her ear, and then looked back at Alice. Clearly she had been expecting someone else. A girlfriend. Not Sandra. Lauren's long honey hair was scrunched on the top of her head. She turned back to Sandra. How do you know Alice? I'm sorry for my rudeness.

Sandra looked at Alice, and Alice understood that she must speak or not speak of it, even though they had not discussed it alone, in advance. Perhaps they did not discuss it when they were alone because their understanding of it, the musings of which were murky even to Alice, was enough. But Alice did not know what Sandra wanted them to be and Alice did not know, either. Or perhaps she knew but did not know whether it was possible, and if not, why. Was it Sandra, Alice, both of them, or someone else, everyone else? Nothing else?

We're friends. Alice heard it come from her mouth, and she saw Sandra nod in agreement, but she was disappointed she had said it and disappointed that Sandra had agreed. She grasped the pages of her story, flattening it. Sandra leaned over and touched her forearm. Good luck. Alice nodded but she did not feel like reading now. She had been excited for Sandra to hear her words, her thoughts, her talent, and to be impressed. But now she wondered what Sandra wanted, why she wanted to be known as friends.

She was glad she did not read the story about the veterinarian. Instead, she read a story she wrote about her father, a true story that had happened to him when he was her age and spending a week at the Grand Canyon camping with his cousin Tom. They had hiked off trail to try to get to the Colorado River, but a high-pressure system had made the canyon like an oven. They ran out of water days before the river, and Tom succumbed to heat stroke and died. Alice's father had made it to the river and, near death himself, had come upon some kayakers, who helped him to safety.

She had felt so close to her father while writing and revising the story, and now that she was reading it all she could think about was that she and Lauren had gone to the Grand Canyon one summer as well, at Alice's urging, to see the place that her father had cheated death before it eventually cheated him. She wondered whether Lauren was thinking the same thing, if it was some kind of signal. But she had not chosen it for Lauren. She had chosen it because it was not about Lauren.

Alice glanced up at Sandra, who was watching her carefully, and she felt braver, happier. Sandra had history, perhaps even wisdom from history, but Alice had talent, so perhaps they could be equals. And more than friends. She began reading.

Sandra rose to her feet when she had finished and smiled. They were alone for a second before Alice's other friends gathered. Alice wanted Sandra to kiss her. Her cheek would suffice. But perhaps it was not in Sandra's history. Sandra who believed that affection was a vice. That was stunning.

Thanks. Alice laced her fingers around Sandra's arm. It really happened to my father.

What a great story, Alice. Lauren had made it to them from the back of the store. Alice and I visited the exact spot where her father and uncle went off trail. It's such an amazing and intimidating place. Isn't it, Alice?

Yes. Alice looked at Sandra, whose eyes were so heavy, so full of so many words. Have you been?

Sandra shook her head, her smile slight. She had not moved from Alice's grasp.

Maybe we can go this summer, you and I, Alice said, even though she knew they would not. There were many things that they would not do. Ski at Vail. Walk the Golden Gate Bridge. Cycle in upstate New York. Horseback ride in Virginia.

I'd like that, Sandra answered. And then Lauren frowned. Lauren looked at Sandra, her water eyes, the triangle of flesh at the base of her neck, Alice's fingers around her arm. Lauren looked at Alice, and Alice could read her thoughts before she thought them. Lauren frowned.

Have you eaten? Lauren asked finally. The gang is going over to Sascha's.

Alice had been to Sascha's with the others before. It was a good time, lots of wine and then some dancing at the X. She looked at Sandra and shook her head. No, we haven't eaten, but we already have dinner plans.

You could come out later, Lauren pressed. After dinner. We'll be at the X, I'm sure.

I won't be free. Thanks, anyway. Lauren and Alice looked at each other and Alice watched Lauren's jaw tighten, her fingers curl.

It was a pleasure to meet you. Sandra held out her hand to Lauren, who took it but did not reply. And when Alice walked out of the bookstore with Sandra, she didn't think about Lauren anymore.

We could have gone with your friends, Sandra said.

It's okay. Alice reached over and threaded her hand into Sandra's. We can eat in.

Are you sure? I don't want to get in the way of the things you like to do.

It's okay. Alice loosened her hand from Sandra's. She put it in her purse, felt her phone, her wallet.

But something... bothers you.

Are we friends? Alice looked out the window. That's all?

Those were your words. Not mine.

But you didn't correct me.

Was I supposed to?

I don't know. I hated to say them, and I hated even more that you agreed.

Alice. Sandra turned in her seat. You have to understand... this is so new to me. And it is not a reflection... of how I feel about you, but how I feel about so many new things. After being alone. And being afraid. And not knowing what is going to happen.

No one knows what's going to happen. That's just how it happens.

But your understanding... of what is appropriate is different from mine. Which may be a hurdle, or we may meet in the middle. But I'm here, now, when it would have been easier to take aspirin and go to bed.

I'm sorry. I don't want to ask more of you than what's comfortable.

You can ask. Sandra smiled. I want you to ask.

Alice did not know what she could give Sandra, how she could care for Sandra. What would she get her for her birthday? Know that during the Nixon administration was when she played her best piano? That she had skied with Georgi before, at the Poconos, and had broken her ankle? The polio?

Your story was wonderful. Sandra's hand moved across the seat, touched Alice's thigh. I mean that. I've done quite a bit of reading—and I think you're going to be something. Do you... have enough stories for a book?

I think so. I'll probably get something together soon.

Can I read it? While you get it together? Maybe you need someone else's opinion, like what goes together and doesn't.

Sure you can read it, Alice laughed. Although I have to warn you, it's about young people.

Well, perhaps stories about young people will help me understand a certain young person better.

Like she wants to go for dinner? Alice laughed. Sandra told the driver to go to Little Italy, to that Italian place everybody liked, and Alice didn't argue.

14.

She was doing too much. The going up to Alice's apartment and the reading and then their trip to the museum the next day and now she was so tired and she wasn't even sure she could get out of bed. It had been many years to this. She had stopped jogging in her fifties, when an overuse injury nagged her hip even then. Then osteoporosis. She tried to jog again and wound up in bed for days. She began to treat her body like glass. If things began to break down, they would not mend. They would forever remain apart, she would become full of chasms, holes, holes bigger than the Grand Canyon. And where would she be, then? In her dreams she saw her mother's hands, fingers twisted over each other like a Twizzler, her sister's bulby knuckles full of arthritis. She was lucky she could still play the piano. When she could not do that, she figured, she would be old.

She was tired and her chest was dull. Alice would not be home from work until seven. Would she come over? She had stayed the weekend and Sandra had bought her a toothbrush, some supplies. When Alice left Sunday night they had kissed and Alice said she would call.

She got up to make coffee but picked up her cell phone and went back to bed. Jack had angina for years. He took the nitroglycerin and she brought him broth, hot tea, in bed. She smoothed his hair, what was left of it. You're working too hard. She patted his cheek. How about we go to Bali? Or even just Maine? He would grunt, turn over, breathing heavy in his pillow. The war was over and they had made their peace and she loved him more than she ever had even though he had not changed. She changed. She was thankful for him. Thankful that he had not divorced her after Leroy, had not tried to take Andrea. That he never cared enough to suspect Georgi. That he gave her his money and let her play the piano and plan the parties and sleep in the same hotel bed when they visited Andrea at Amherst. She changed and now she didn't want him to leave so soon. It would have been the same, ten more years, twenty, of their uneasy peace, but it would have been enough.

She thought about the Grand Canyon. Would the air be suffocating? Would the sun burn her cheeks, her shoulders, shoulders that had not seen the sun in years, skin hungry for touch and warmth and sun? She thought of Alice's hair caught in a hot gust, her toothy smile, dimples, a hotel bed. A shared tube of toothpaste.

She listened for Andrea's voice on the line, heard a swooshing instead. She was in the car, coming or going.

My chest hurts.

Jesus, Mom. Are you lying down?

Yes. It's like your father's.

Have you been to the doctor?

No. It could be indigestion. She thought of the lasagna, so rich, the ricotta, the Chianti for dinner Saturday. The sticky buns and bagels Alice had gotten from the bakery on Sunday morning. They sat in bed with the window open and Alice traced her finger on Sandra's collarbone, her shoulder, her neck. Alice's lips touched hers, and Sandra's heart fluttered, fluttered like a bird. Not like this.

Mom, I want you to call an ambulance.

I don't want to, yet. I just wanted to let you know.

Mom, I'm going to call.

Sandra hung up the phone. Of course Andrea would overreact. Maybe if she lived closer she would not. If the paramedics came she would tell them she felt fine. A little indigestion. She would wait for Alice. Sandra would take a nap, and then when Alice got off work she would be fine. She dialed Alice's number and got her voicemail. Please come over tonight, if you can. It's important. And then she pulled the blankets over her head, breathed heavy in the pillow.

* * *

The knock scared her. It was far and then close and then far and then the men were there, men in blue with crosses on their jackets asking her questions and she couldn't answer because someone had hit her in the chest so hard she couldn't breathe.

They put her in the ambulance. When Jack died it had been so sudden. He stood in the kitchen smelling his coffee and then he frowned at her before collapsing. The coffee cup splintered and sliced his palm and she pressed his hand, full of blood, closed as she tried to give CPR like she learned at the Y. Breathe, Jack. Please. She screamed for the neighbors before getting up and calling the ambulance. Keep breathing, Jack. Keep your eyes open. His eyes were open but they did not look at her. The red/white flash of lights filled the kitchen. She leaned down and kissed his cheek before the paramedics crowded her away from him. When she came home that evening, alone, Jack's clothes in a plastic bag, she sat in the kitchen and listened to the answering machine, Andrea's flight still two hours away. She sat in the kitchen with the wall phone smeared with blood and the coffee dried black and red on the tiles and she sat there, afraid to move, until Andrea came.

She woke up in a bed with a tube in her arm and a piano on her chest. Something beeping, in addition to her heart, still beating. He sat in the chair wearing that woolen suit that strained across his stomach with the pilled red sweater vest he loved so much. You're all right, dear. He wiped his glasses on his shirt cuff. Just a little heart attack.

Take me home. She moved to sit up but the weight on her was too heavy. Take me home, Jack.

She found the button connected to the cord and pressed it. When the nurse came she asked her to check for Jack in the bathroom. Could he have gone down to the cafeteria? Picked up Andrea? Who, Mrs. Holiday? The nurse inflated her arm with the blood pressure cuff. She needed to call Alice. Is Alice your daughter? The nurse took her temperature. Has someone contacted my daughter? I don't know, ma'am. The only person who knew she was here was Jack and he was gone. She closed her eyes, convinced she would wake up at home. A dream.

But when she awoke her sister was on the bed. She brushed her hair, long, blond. Like Sandra's once. Before Sandra got tired of dyeing it, combing over the thin spots, and cut it all off. Sandy, you're all right. Clarice smiled. She had cheeks like a kewpie doll. She had both breasts but was a sunken shell, like when she died. Just a little heart attack, Sandy.

But Clarice, it hurts so much.

Better to hurt and be alive, Sandy. Mom says hi.

Mom, who are you talking to? Andrea took Sandra's hand.

Clarice. Sandra pointed.

Oh, Mom. Andrea kissed her. Oh, Mom. Shh. They gave you medicine. You're just dreaming.

You need to get in touch with Alice, please.

Who's Alice?

My Alice. Please. My phone.

Don't worry Mom—I have a copy of your insurance. I took care of everything. Just rest. You're going to be fine.

I need to talk to Alice.

Just get some sleep, Mom.

Sandra closed her eyes and when she awoke Jack and Clarice were gone but Andrea was still there.

Mom, you should eat something. Andrea pushed a spoon of oatmeal toward her.

Did Alice call? Did you check my phone?

Mom, I don't know who Alice is. Andrea pulled her hair, long, blond, up in a ponytail. Who's Alice?

Alice. She helps me with the blog.

Oh, Alice. Andrea stirred Sandra's oatmeal. Don't worry. I'll let her know you can't do the blog right now.

You need to tell her I'm here.

I will.

I need to see her.

You need your rest. Andrea patted her arm. You can see all your friends when you feel better.

Dammit. Sandra sat up in bed. If you're not going to call her, get me a phone.

Mom, I'll call her, okay? Just calm down—you want to have another heart attack?

How bad was it? Sandra looked at her food. Perhaps if she had not had those honey buns, had so much coffee.

It wasn't good, Mom, but you'll be okay. Just take it easy.

I don't want to live with you, Andrea. I want to go home. To my place. You understand?

Sure, Mom. You'll be home again.

Don't lie to me. When Andrea had come after Jack died and saw the blood, the coffee, she dropped her purse on the floor and started to cry. Sandra stood and touched her, put her hand on her cheek. I know, baby, I know. But Andrea pushed her way. Jesus, Mom. She bent to pick up the shards of mug. Couldn't you clean this up before I got here? Did I have to see this?

15.

During her break Alice left Sandra a message, telling her she'd
stop by after work. After work she took the bus home and got
in the shower. She pulled a bag out from under the bed and put
a change of clothes in it. She wondered whether she was being
presumptuous. She took the clothes out and put the bag back
under the bed. She fingered the mail and called Sandra again and
got her voicemail. She picked up the stories she printed out and
put them in her shoulder bag. On the bus she wondered whether
Sandra would like to have dinner. She could stop at the store,
if only Sandra would call back. Sandra's stop came and Alice
buzzed Sandra on the intercom. She buzzed her again and then
opened her phone and called but it went right into voicemail.
She waited for someone to come and open the door and then
she slipped inside and took the stairs up to Sandra's floor. She
knocked and put her ear to the door. She pulled out her phone
and listened to Sandra's message. She wondered if she should
alert the management, ask them to open Sandra's apartment.
Perhaps Sandra was just out at the store.

She sat down by the door and pulled out her stories and read over them. After the fifth story she wondered whether she could sneak a cigarette but she would have to slip back into the building again. It was almost eight and she was starving. She had ten dollars in her account until payday the day after tomorrow; she could not take the bus home and come back, unless she borrowed fare. She would have to go home and eat there, wait for Sandra to call. If Sandra wanted her to come back, she could send the car.

At home she had a cup of yogurt and waited for Sandra to call. It was ten.

Sandra, please call me back. She left another message. If you're scared or worried, let's talk about it. And if you're worried about me, you shouldn't be. I want to see you again. I want to see you all the time. I want to see you tonight.

She pulled the phone book out and ran her finger down the area hospitals. She shut the book and surfed the Internet and waited. When her father died, she had been sleeping. She and her mother had been at the hospital for thirty-five hours when her mother had Alice take a taxi home so she could walk Silkie, feed the cats. She walked Silkie and fed the cats and sat on the couch with Silkie and was too tired to cry, too tired to go upstairs to bed. She sat on the couch and she tried to remember the Lord's Prayer and Silkie laid her head on Alice's lap and went to sleep. When Alice woke up, the phone was ringing. It was light outside and she thought it was too cliché for her mother to be calling that Alice's father just died. But she started to cry anyway because it was true.

She opened the phone book and began to call. And when they confirmed that yes, a Sandra Holiday was admitted to Greater Baltimore Medical Center she took the emergency twenty dollars she kept in her yarn basket and called a cab.

Are you family? The hospital clerk asked.

No—but her family lives out of state.

I'm sorry. Visiting hours are over tonight. The clerk picked up the phone. She looked over the receiver at Alice. They start at eleven tomorrow.

Alice went to the lobby and sat on the couch. She called the bookstore and told them she would not be in the next day. She had spent twelve dollars for the cab and needed three dollars for the bus home, which would give leave her five dollars. But she could not eat. She tucked her bag underneath her, her knees on the couch, and leaned her head back. She was used to sleeping at the hospital. She liked that someone was always awake. She liked that someone was watching over her father when she and her mother could not. Don't be so glum. The tube cold arm of her father held her hand. You'll always be my boo-girl. The liquid dripped into the tube arm, replacing her father. She slept in chairs and on couches and ate chips from the vending machine. Why hadn't she told Sandra about her father when she asked?

She would call her mother but it was late and what would she say? She closed her eyes and wondered if Sandra had broken her hip, if she had a stroke or cancer. Alice had not stopped loving her father but she was not sure what she would be for Sandra or what Sandra would be for her. She cried a little. She walked through the lobby. She wondered if she looked in all the doorways whether she would see Sandra in one of them. She walked through the tunnels of green and tan and pink walls and counted her steps as she walked past rooms of people sleeping. Some of them would die but she hoped not Sandra. Would it always be this way with Sandra? If not tonight, maybe next week?

Are you lost? The nurse stood up from the station and followed her a few steps.

I'm looking for my mother.

She followed the nurse back to the desk and she watched the nurse type in Sandra Holiday. She's in the cardiology wing, dear. You have to go down two floors and go to the extension.

There was a woman in Sandra's room, her blond hair pulled in a ponytail. A younger Sandra. Alice stood at the edge of the doorway, holding her bag.

Can I help you? The woman came to the door. She frowned, magazine in her hand.

I came to see Sandra.

She's asleep, and it's late. The woman turned toward the bed, and Alice could see the white of Sandra's hair on the pillow. Who are you?

I'm Alice.

The women's brow scrunched, her eyes darting back and forth. She sighed, softly. My mother had a little heart attack, but she's fine. I'll let her know you stopped by.

How did it happen?

She had some chest pains and called me and I called the ambulance. The woman blocked the door. I'm sorry, but it's very late.

Alice wondered if Andrea knew. She walked down the halls of the extension. She could find her way to the reception area but she did not see the point in sleeping there. Alice's mother did not know, either. Lauren knew. But Alice and Sandra didn't even know what they were to each other. But she was here. And she thought that should count for something.

16.

She did not know how many days it had been. Sometimes it was light out when she woke up, and sometimes it was dark. Sometimes the shadows crept across the home decorating shows on the television, anchored from the ceiling, that Andrea watched, and sometimes everything was etched clear, scrubbed and shiny and cold. Sandra ate soup and yogurt and chicken. There were medicines to take when she got home and follow-up appointments with her cardiologist.

Have you called Alice? Sandra asked Andrea. She asked her when the shadows were long and the shadows were short and when she felt nauseous and when she felt sad. She did not feel happy. It seemed like only time now, treading water until the deep plunge, never to surface.

I left her a message, Mom. Andrea was knitting a cap. For Elvin or Beatrice, Sandra was not sure. And why, since they lived in Florida.

Did you check my messages? On my cell? She would be happy if Alice came. Someone to keep her afloat. Alice's dimples and lively eyes and curled line of hip and small breasts and her warm soft seal skin pressed against hers, under the covers, protecting her from the shadows stretching across the space.

Yes, Mom.

You don't understand. Alice is very important to me. I shall be very upset if you've been keeping her away.

Mom, please rest. Andrea cupped her hand on top of Sandra's. And then when you're better you can run around with your friends.

If she could get to a phone she could call Alice herself or the driver and have him take her to the bookstore or Alice's apartment. But maybe if she was quiet and took her medicines, ate her meals, and pinched her cheeks pink they would let her go home and she could see Alice.

I am going home, Andrea. She scraped the last of the peas onto her fork even though she hated them.

Yes, Mom. Andrea left for hours each day to eat, to call her husband, her children, to make arrangements. Andrea would stay with Sandra for a week, and then what? She wouldn't say.

The shadows striped her bed, her hands. She would be going home soon. But she knew there would be shadows there too.

17.

Alice went to work. At break she called Sandra's number but her messages went into voicemail and after work she took the bus and snuck into the building and sat by Sandra's door. She tried to write Sandra a letter, but she didn't know what to say. She sat by the door and wondered what she would say if she heard footsteps inside, voices. Had Andrea told Sandra she had come? Did Sandra not want to see her?

Lauren called her one night and Alice met her at the movie theater. They watched a movie and had a coffee and laughed about a memory involving a stray dog they had taken in for the night into their old apartment. Lauren did not ask about Sandra and Alice did not tell her. Alice was happy not to be alone. She was happy when Lauren came over and they listened to old CDs and shared a clove cigarette. And she remembered all the things she liked about Lauren, the way she laughed, the way she crossed her legs, easily and confidently, the way she asked about Alice's mother. The way she stirred her coffee and held a magazine in one hand, reading standing up. The way she would kiss Alice's forehead in the morning when she left for school, the way she'd trace circles in Alice's back at night until she fell asleep.

Alice went to work and then she took the bus to her place and waited outside. She opened a book and sat down on the sidewalk just as the blond-haired woman, Sandra's daughter, walked up with some plastic shopping bags.

I'd like to see Sandra. Alice stood up. Just for a few minutes.

The woman, Andrea, stared at her with Sandra's water eyes. Her shoulders slumped as she fumbled for the door key.

All right. She thrust the key in the lock and jiggled it. But you can't stay long. My mother is still weak.

She followed Andrea up to the apartment. Some of the furniture was missing. Boxes rested on the sofa.

You can't tell her about this. Andrea motioned toward the boxes. She doesn't know yet.

Alice walked toward the bedroom. It was the bedroom she had slept in with Sandra and shared breakfast in but it was different. It was because of the light or the clutter or Sandra, lying so still in bed, her eyes closed. Alice sat on the bed and touched Sandra's knee through the bedspread.

Where have you been? Sandra's eyes opened. She pushed herself up.

Why haven't you called me back?

Close the door, please.

Alice closed the door and came back to the bed.

Oh Alice. It was all Sandra said before she started to cry. Alice held her and Sandra cried, so much water, her body shaking. Alice.

I'm so sorry, Sandra.

I'll be fine. Sandra shook her head, wiped her eyes, nose. It was a little heart attack. I should be up and about tomorrow. I'll be fine.

Don't rush. Alice patted her thigh. So thin, she thought maybe she could touch the bone.

You're not going to have to take care of me. Sandra drank some water from a glass by the bedside. I would never ask that.

And you would never do that, I know. And that's all right.

I could move in. Alice took the glass from Sandra and replaced it on the bedside table. Sandra patted the bed.

Come here.

I can't—

Andrea can go to hell. Sandra pulled back the sheet. But Alice did not move. She heard Andrea moving around in the kitchen, the coffee pot percolating.

Do you want some coffee? Alice looked at her hands.

I can't have any. Sandra sighed, dabbed her eyes. You don't have to stay here. You don't have to worry about me. I'm sure you've got things to do.

I'll stay until Andrea makes me leave.

You're my guest. You can stay as long as you want.

There seemed to be nothing to say except for all the things they couldn't say.

You won't leave, will you? Sandra clutched the sheets around her.

When you get tired, I'll go.

I'll never get tired of you.

You could get tired in five years. Alice smiled.

I might be dead in five years. Sandra smiled. But I'll understand... if you don't want to continue.

Continue us? Alice put her hands on Sandra's thighs. Don't be silly. I've been crazy, trying to find out if you were all right.

Mom. Andrea opened the door and Alice stood up. Mom, I've got some soup and salad for you.

Just leave it here by the bed. Sandra patted the night table. Andrea put it down and sighed.

Mom, I don't want you to spend all your energy chit-chatting.

Why don't you run your errands? Sandra unfolded a napkin. Alice can stay with me.

Fine. Andrea looked at Alice. Just leave the dishes in the sink. I doubt you know where everything goes.

They listened to the front door slam. Sandra laughed, blew on her chicken soup.

Have you told her? Alice walked to the other side of the bed and carefully sat down.

In so many words. If you're hungry, please fix yourself something. You haven't eaten yet, have you?

No. Do you mind? Alice kissed Sandra's cheek and went to the kitchen. She found some turkey and some bread and some mustard and a can of Fanta and when she heard Sandra curse she ran out into the living room.

Where are my things?

I don't think you should be up. Alice wrapped her arms around Sandra, but she shook her off.

Did you know about this? Sandra's eyes were wild.

Andrea said...

What, you're both lying to me? Sandra slapped her. Are you both in cahoots to send me to some nursing home in Florida to die?

Sandra. Alice touched her face where it burned. I had no idea. I had no idea.

I'm sorry. Sandra touched Alice's cheek. I'm so sorry, Alice. Forgive me. Sandra brought Alice to her, kissed her. I didn't mean that. I didn't expect my things to be gone, my life.

She can't make you do anything. Alice walked over to one of the boxes and opened it. She pulled out a vase. Where should this go?

But Sandra did not answer. Tears ran down her face. When Alice stood up Sandra limped back toward the bedroom. Alice brought in her sandwich. They ate.

18.

I didn't want to upset you, Mom. Andrea washed dishes in the kitchen. You're too fragile to be upset.

All you've done since you've come is upset me. On the sofa Sandra pulled her sheet music out of a box by her feet. Andrea came from the kitchen, running her hands through her hair. First you keep Alice from visiting. And then you try to move me out without even telling me.

I didn't have to come up here. Your precious Alice could have taken off work instead, sat with you for three days. Why even contact me? And when you die Alice can make your funeral arrangements for you, too.

Now you're being cruel.

And you're acting like a child. Don't you see how foolish you're being? Andrea sat down next to her.

No, please tell me. Mozart's Piano Concerto No. 9. Chopin's Etude in D Minor. A Little Night Music. She spread them across the coffee table. Is it the fact that it's someone younger, a woman, or both?

What are you expecting is going to happen? Andrea lifted her mug from the coffee table. It sloshed against the rim, droplets escaping and absorbing into the carpet. Sandra squeezed her tissue in her robe pocket. You expect to set up house with this Alice? Put her through college? If she's even thought that far ahead, which I doubt, she's probably planning to squeeze you dry.

Don't worry, Andrea. Sandra patted her thigh. *Your* money's safe.

That's not what I'm worried about. Andrea shook her head. She stared across the top of her coffee mug. Andrea had started to hate her in high school, Sandra was sure. When the pieces, memories of her youth started to find the spokes and holes of each other. The jigsaw was laid. Sandra in the middle, Leroy and Georgi and herself in the murky corners. I'm worried about your state of mind, Mom. I just don't know what you're thinking. At least your hatred of Daddy, it all makes sense now.

Don't reduce it to such simplicity. Do you think I planned to care for Alice?

I know you've cared for others.

Maybe you shouldn't talk. She squeezed the tissue harder. Of things about which you know nothing.

I know more than you think. Sandra studied her from the corner of her eye.

Well, please, then—let me know exactly how I can be a good mother to you, Andrea, since I failed so utterly.

Who's cruel now? Andrea dabbed her eye with her pinky. How do you think I felt, when you woke up in the hospital, that the first person you asked for was Alice? After I spent the day getting the kids to Dan's mother's, packing, getting a flight on standby, doing all your insurance information, and you, you ask for Alice. Alice!

Sandra bit her lip, reached over and laid her arm across Andrea's shoulders.

I'm sorry. Her hand closed around Andrea's arm. She is all I have here.

It's not an option. Andrea stood up with her mug. Staying here is not an option I'm giving you. If I leave here without you, you're on your own. And Alice will be all you have.

My memories. Sandra gathered the sheet music and put it back in the box. They're here, too.

You can have memories anywhere. Sandra stood and went to the piano, sat down. She spread her fingers, let them hover over the keys. They did not stretch as far as they once did. She moved through chord progressions, triads, the eighths.

Andrea sat down beside her, touched her shoulder.

You can take the piano, Mom. She dabbed the tears from Sandra's eyes. Of course.

19.

Alice stocked books. She helped a woman wearing pajama bottoms find a book about unlocking the secrets to one's life. Alice thought of herself wearing silk pajamas, a robe, to work, bunny slippers. Perhaps she would bring her pillow, too. She thought of Sandra, so carefully clothed, her waist surrounded by belts, pleats. The cuffs of her shirts. Alice unpacked boxes from distributors. She ran her hands over identical covers. Maybe she could get a teaching job in Florida. Her friends would question her. They would be tactful, of course. They would remind her that her life was open, and that she should go where opportunity presented itself to her, not to someone else. They would be right, except they didn't love this woman. Perhaps it was too early to think about love. Perhaps it was too late to think about love.

On her break Alice called Sandra. She would not have moved to Vancouver, Lauren was right. Because of her mother or because of Lauren, she was not sure. She got Sandra's voicemail. I hope you're well. Is it all right to see you?

After work Alice went home and ate yogurt, toast. She called her mother.

I'm baking Dutch apple pies. She heard the television in the background. Why don't you come home this weekend, help me peel?

A friend is sick. Alice held the phone away from her face, swallowed air forcefully, unevenly. Can I let you know?

Honey, you're breaking up. Her mother echoed. Can you call back?

Can you come get me after work tomorrow? She asked, before the line cut out, before she started crying. Before she turned the phone off.

She slept in her bed in her old room under the Smiths poster that her mother had never taken down. Her mother was superstitious after her father's death. Time stopped and Alice's mother stopped but she kept living, baking pies. Sometimes Alice felt far away from her, and sometimes she felt close. She felt far away now, under the comforter smelling like home, like fresh laundering.

What would you do if I moved away? Alice cored and cut the apples slowly, unlike her mother, whose hands, plump and mottled, moved like a machine. The slithers of skin fell around Alice's fingers, curls of green with pale meat.

Are you interviewing for a job? Her mother felled the apples. They split in quarters, in eighths. She put the slices in a bowl.

Maybe. Florida.

That's so far away. Her mother frowned. She still dyed her hair. It was dark against her face. She slept in curlers and combed it out in the morning.

It's two hours by plane.

Of course, I should be thrilled for you. A real teaching job. Her mother smiled, her eyes on the apples.

Would you have moved far from your mother for Dad?

I don't know. Her mother sighed. It's hard to say now. But your father loved Pennsylvania. His whole family is here. I don't think he would have wanted to move, at any rate. But you should do what makes you happy.

But that was the problem, Alice thought. Happiness was always at the expense of someone else.

She lay in her old room under her old posters and called Sandra. Please call me back. Let me know when I can see you. She pulled the covers over her head and called Lauren.

20.

She wrote Alice a letter. If she saw her it would be too hard. She used her old stationary with her embossed monogram. *When I first began this project with you, I had no expectations. I anticipated overpaying for someone to romanticize my life for my grandchildren. And perhaps for me. I don't know, at times it has felt so trivial, but then I think of the sorrows and joys of my life, it has probably been as rich as anyone else's. I talk as if it has already ended. I realize, by my feelings for you, that it has not. You are a lovely, beautiful woman, and I am not ashamed to say that as I listened to you read that night in the bookstore that I fell in love with you. I should probably not tell you these things, as my circumstances, such as they are, have convinced me that it would be unfair to you to pursue a relationship. In light of my situation, I have decided to move closer to my daughter, who is more prepared and more obligated to care for me should I need help. Please do not take this as an indictment of your capabilities. You are young and are in a position to take advantage of great opportunities by virtue of your great talent.*

And please know that I expect no less of you. Thank you for everything. I will always remember it. To desire, to feel desired. You've given so much to me. Yours, Sandra. She included a check for two-hundred dollars, what she imagined the remainder of their sessions might cost, and the remaining symphony tickets for the season.

It was getting colder now. She played the piano, a little bit at a time. Until she got her strength. Haydn and Gershwin and Mozart. Mozart for Jack, always. No Beethoven. She played the piano while the women Andrea hired packed her things, while the men took her furniture. She played the piano until they were ready to take it, and when they did, she left.

21.

It came on a Tuesday. She had expected the news but not the letter. She opened it and studied the monogram, the tight script. She read the letter and then she read it again, sitting down. She did not get up for a long time. When she did, she threw the check in the trash along with the tickets but then thought better of it. She put the check in her yarn basket.

It had not been a long time. Them. A few months. In a few months she would take the bus to the other part of town, and the name on apartment 12B's call number would not be Holiday. And she would cry still. In a few more months she would take over the teaching load of an associate professor out sick. And, a few months after that, she would meet Janie. But right now she could not think a few months ahead, a few minutes ahead. She could not think of anything except Sandra's eyes, her fingers on the keys. She looked for the piano in the classifieds, on Craigslist, thought somehow she would buy it. She framed the picture of Sandra in the Hamptons and put it on